The Hookman Legacy

By

Hayley Bernard

© COPYRIGHT 2015

SNM NOVEL PUBLICATIONS

*ALL RIGHTS RESERVED

ISBN# 978-1511499866

Contextual Edits - Layout: Steven Marshall

Grammar - Text Editing: Sarah Butler

Cover Art - Front and Back: Pavarti Tyler

Published by SNM Book Publishing in 2015

Copyright © Hayley Bernard

Check out our website:

www.snmhorrormag.com

Table of Contents

Ghosts in the Closet......................................1

Treeface and Tobias.....................................8

Swamp Turtles and Silver Eggs................. 19

The Firehouse Dance....................................30

The Frog Pond... 45

The Fading of Zachary.................................55

The Farmhouse Witches.............................. 67

Indian Myths and Curses............................80

The Oxoboxo River Ghosts.........................96

The Centaur and The Prophet..................118

The Hookman Legacy.................................132

The Return of Remus................................. 149

For My Family

CHAPTER ONE
Ghosts in the Closet

THE FIRST DAY OF SPRING in 1990 marked the first encounter Lynn Strauss experienced with a ghost.

But not the last...

It was shortly after midnight. Lynn was lying on her bed, staring at the ceiling, dreading her math test the next morning, when her closet door began to glow with a fierce orange light.

Lynn noticed the change in lighting in her room and turned her head to look at the glowing closet door.

Her heart began pounding hard in her chest. She remained stiff as a board on her bed, unable to move or even cry out.

The lights slowly pierced through the cracks of the door frame, pulsating alive, as if morphing from yellow to orange to red in gradual phases of the color spectrum.

"Lynn-iiieee," sang out the cold, whispering voice behind the door.

Lynn stammered. Her face flushed white as she sat up in the bed and peeled the covers off her body with shaking fingers.

She had to leave the room and get her Daddy. He would know what to do. Lynn hadn't called her father 'Daddy' since she was little.

Now, at practically twelve-years old, she was nearly a teenager, and her father was just 'Dad,' which was the grown-up way to say it.

"Lynn-iiieee...open the door-"

Right now, however, with her sheets soaked in a cold sweat, her face the color of the white nightgown her mom bought for her on her last birthday, she saw some mysterious light calling out to her to open her closet door, and felt more vulnerable and helpless than at any point in her life.

"Lynn!" the voice beckoned.

No way. This isn't happening.

"Go away!" Lynn asserted, her hands flying over her ears.

The light glowed brighter and the entire room shook and rattled.

An unearthly wailing noise resounded from behind the door, which quaked on its hinges.

Odd knickknacks fell off the shelves, books flew out of her bookcase, and slammed into the far side wall as Bedtime Bear rolled off her lap and landed on the hardwood floor.

"Stooop!" Lynn screamed, squeezing her eyes shut.

A second later, the room became silent. Lynn could only hear the sounds of her own ragged breathing and the frantic thumping of her heart, which pounded like a trapped rabbit in a cage. What would she see if she opened her eyes?

What if the thing was sitting right in front of her, staring at her through its liquid obsidian eyes...waiting to chomp into her face with its razor-sharp teeth?

Her eyes sprang open. Nothing. There was nothing there. The dark house held within it the silence of a grave. The closet door was bathed in shadows cast from the full moon that shone into her room. The eerie light was gone.

Lynn heaved a huge sigh of relief. She leaned over to retrieve her fallen comrade, Bedtime Bear, from the floor. He held his little furry arms out to her as if to say, "Hold me and everything will be alright," and that's just what she wanted to do.

That is, until she could build enough courage to bolt from her room and wake her father.

Lynn's hair stood up on end and her breath got caught in her throat. Bedtime Bear slipped from her shaky fingers and landed in her lap. The closet door was wide open. Standing in front of it were two little Indian girls, wallowing in the fierce, yellow lights that shone out of the closet space behind them. They stared at her through glowing eyes the color of hot searing flames.

Eleven-year old Lynn, who was never at a loss for words before now, found herself completely speechless. Her closed-up throat only released a petrified squeak.

The girls' dark hair flew around them in a haze of pulsating energy. When they spoke, their lips moved at the same time and their voices blended together like music. "He's coming," they said, remorsefully. The Indian girl on the left was the soprano, her identical twin on the right spoke in low, alto tones.

Lynn's knuckles were as white as her hands clutching around her bedspread. She remained motionless and stared hard at the twins through disbelieving eyes, wide as half-dollar coins.

Go away. Please, please go away.

The apparitions either could not probe inside her mind or worse, they could, and ignored her request. "He's coming," they repeated, this time louder and with more urgency than before.

It was at this point that Lynn realized she was probably dreaming. Yep, that had to be it. There were no such things as ghosts, except in books or the movies.

She was dreaming of the orange-eyed Indian girls because she stayed up late with her older sister, Carly. They watched "Poltergeist" and ate popcorn too late at night. That had to be it. Yet... the Indian girls looked so *real.*

The cold air sweeping across the room felt pretty real, too. Lynn reached a shaking hand up to her opposite arm and gave it a good pinch. Chills and goosebumps enveloped her flesh.

The Indian girls glided forward from several feet above the ground to the edge of the bed.

"No, please, no-" Lynn whispered, tearfully.

The apparitions halted and looked down on her as she sat there.

"You are Lynn Strauss," they asked in unison in overlapping voices.

Lynn wasn't certain if it was a question or a statement. At the moment, she wasn't even quite sure what was real anymore.

"Y-Yes," she choked.

"Then you are the one," the girls said eerily, their mechanical voices singing out as one. "The Hookman has killed for the last time. You are the one to banish him from this place. It is time."

Lynn wasn't sure what they meant. Hookman? What in the name of Jesus and all things holy was a Hookman? And what did this have to do with her?

How did these ghosts, or whatever they were, get inside her closet? Why were they dressed in strange brown dresses with feathers sticking out of their braids? What did they want her to do? All these questions built up inside her head, but all she could manage to do is squeak out was a high-pitched, "Huh?"

The two girls smiled for the first time. Their mouths were closed and their grins remained tight-lipped.

If they bared any teeth, even if it was just to smile, Lynn was sure she'd have a heart attack on the spot.

"**You are the one**," the sisters whispered in perfect unison, gliding backwards into the closet. "**Kill The Hookman**," their voices trailed off as the lights around them glowed brighter and they started to fade. "Set us free."

Then they were gone in a mere blink.

Lynn blinked and the closet door was shut.

The room was dark and silent once more.

*

CHAPTER TWO
Treeface and Tobias

LYNN PEDALED HARD down Old Colchester Road. She reached the store down the hill and made a sharp left onto the paved road that led to Camp Oakdale.

She wheeled right past the street sign without catching its name and silently cursed herself. She always wanted to know what this road was called, but always drove by the sign too fast to catch the name.

Her legs were already feeling very sore from pumping the pedals of her bicycle so hard, but she didn't mind one bit. Riding her bike down the country roads and dirt trails of Montville was one of her favorite escapes.

Lynn's mother, Christine Strauss, had always advised her to stay in the Manor or on the roads close to it. According to Lynn, however, "close" had the capacity for a broader range of meaning and she often went further than her mother had recommended.

Lynn lived on New York Rd. in the Montville Manor. Three of her best friends, Devon, Andrea, and Laurie, lived on Rhode Island, Texas, and Georgia Road nearby.

Lynn loved the fact that the Manor streets were named after states. She felt cooler writing out envelopes with her address being New York Rd. She knew she lived in the northern state of Connecticut, a word she could never for the life of her spell right, but it was fun to pretend.

Lynn reached the end of the long, winding road and stopped by the orange fence. She put one foot on the ground to balance the bike and used her other foot to put down the kickstand.

She needed to take a breather. She wiped the sweat from her face with the beach towel which hung around her neck. She frowned and looked down at the brightly colored fish on the towel.

Darn. She had taken the wrong one. If any of the kids at the camp saw her with a smiling fish towel at her age, she would certainly never hear the end of it.

Lynn shrugged it off. She'd just lay the towel fishy-side-down on the sand and hoped no one would be the wiser.

She reached into the cup-holder and pulled out her water bottle. The cool water soothed her dry throat and cracked lips.

Oh, darn! She forgot to bring her Chapstick again. Oh well, she'd have to do without for the time being.

Why was she always so forgetful?

Devon often joked that Lynn would probably lose her head if it wasn't already attached. Lynn found herself regretfully agreeing that she was probably right.

The loud bang of a series of gunshots firing disturbed the quiet of the forests around her.

Lynn glanced across the street and surveyed the sign: Quaker Hill Gun Club.

She swished the water around her mouth, staring at the sign with a raised eyebrow, then spat the water onto the pavement. She wiped her mouth with the back of her hand and felt almost like Clint Eastwood.

This would be the most dangerous part of the journey. She had to make a right down Camp Oakdale Rd. She knew it wasn't the real name of the road, but she called it that since she always forgot to check the darn street sign.

She'd pedal as fast as she could past the firing range without getting shot. She knew the hunters were really aiming at targets deep in the woods and, most likely, never aimed in the direction of the road.

What if one made a mistake?

What if one of the hunters was crazy?

Lynn squinted her eyes against the glare of the sun's rays and nodded solemnly. *Go ahead,* she thought to the hunters...*Make my day.*

She revved up her purple and pink ten-speed bicycle, which was a sleek, fully loaded Harley Davidson, and barreled a hard right onto Camp Oakdale Rd. with loud gunshot blasts sounding all around her.

The tall oaks that lined the road swayed in the light afternoon breeze.

"Lynn-iiieee," the voice sang out. The sound sailed through the wind and whispered through the tree branches.

"What the-" Lynn thought, confused. She had to be hearing things again. What happened the other night was just a dream. This couldn't be happening now. Certainly not when she was wide awake and outdoors.

Suddenly, the tree branches hanging over the road in front of her wove together and created a glaring face that stared down at her menacingly. "Lynn!" the Leaf Face screamed in a loud, deep voice. The wind took up the branches and the face snarled and separated.

Lynn shrieked. Her towel slipped from her neck and got caught in the wheel spokes on the front tire. The bicycle, which had been going 10 MPH, came to an abrupt halt.

Lynn flew over the handlebars and landed hard on her right elbow. She cried out in pain as the loose gravel skinned her knee. She stayed on the ground for a moment, breathing heavily, then slowly sat up to assess the damage.

Remembering the voice, Lynn surveyed the forest around her, but everything seemed normal.

She turned her elbow over to look at the underside of her arm. A gross loose flap of skin dangled and underneath the layer was a bloody gash. Her knee stung, but that cut wasn't as deep.

With her hands shaking, she reached out to pry her towel out from the wheel spokes. A tear trickled down her cheek as she stared at the oil-stained fish towel. This was a new beach towel.

Her mom was going to kill her. That is, if the voice and the Tree Face didn't first. Lynn pulled out the last of the towel from the wheel, quickly lifted the bike to its riding position, hopped on, and took off. She could wash off in the pond.

Lynn made a right into the gravel parking lot of the Camp Oakdale Arts and Crafts building. She was in a bad mood now. She parked her bike in her usual spot around the back of the building and walked around the white-stoned structure to go through the front doors.

Before entering the building, she squinted her eyes across the street at the Pavilion to the fields surrounding the picnic area. It looked like Field Day. She found herself missing camp, even though she told her parents she was too old for it and hated every minute of it. She only stopped going last year.

She watched the kids hopping along in the potato sack race and saw the big crowd cheering them on. That was her best event. Lynn liked to race. She'd have to join cross-country once she got to Murphy Jr. High. She was a lowly fifth-grader at Oakdale Elementary School. She let out a grand sigh. *One more year*. She couldn't wait.

Lynn went through the door and entered the building, clutching her injured arm. She hoped none of the camp counselors or the kids saw her.

She was in no mood to be fussed over. She covered the gash with her hand and winced. Boy, did it sting. Lynn used her other arm to push open the bathroom door and went inside.

The brown paper towel dispenser was next to the sink and she lifted her left hand from the cut to push the lever down.

"Oh, man!" Lynn huffed as she noticed her bloody fingertips on the dispenser. Now she'd have to clean the dispenser too.

Lynn angrily tore off the long sheet of towel and turned on the water to wet it in the sink. She applied the wet paper to her exposed skin and gritted her teeth.

But she refused to cry. Clint Eastwood never cried, neither did Indiana Jones.

And they got beat up *a lot.*

The door swung open and a little girl walked in. She looked about six or seven. Lynn smiled at her and she smiled back. The girl pointed at the paper towel on Lynn's arm.

"You got a boo-boo," the girl observed.

Lynn nodded and continued to smile, even though she'd despised the word "boo-boo". The scrape on her arm was a bloody, gushing, nasty gash - not a boo-boo. She wondered if she should correct the girl.

"Yeah, I got a boo-boo," Lynn affirmed to appease the girl.

The girl clicked her tongue, sympathetically, and walked over to a bathroom stall. "That's too bad," she said. "Feel better!"

"Thanks," Lynn said, feeling more foolish by the minute.

The little girl shut the stall door and Lynn left the bathroom. As she walked down the aisle to the front doors, she found herself surveying the children drawing and coloring at the art tables. All the pictures seemed to have a summer theme.

Lynn smiled. The pictures were really cute. She saw one little girl drawing a beach scene and wished it was summer right now. Her gaze swept to the next table and she froze in her tracks.

The blond haired boy in front of her clutched a silver crayon in his hand and used it to color in the large hook he drew on the white construction paper.

Scrawled in a messy handwriting with a red crayon at the bottom of the page was the name, Tobias.

Lynn knelt over, next to him, looking past his shoulder.

"Hi, what're you drawing?" Lynn asked him.

Tobias didn't look up. "...The Hookman," he said, flatly.

Lynn tried to swallow, but her throat was dry. "Who's that?" she asked.

"Oh you know," the boy said, still emotionless. "The Hookman."

No, she didn't know. But, she'd been hearing enough about him lately.

Too much for her own comfort.

"Have you ever seen him?" Lynn carefully asked.

The boy stayed silent and continued to color.

"What does he do?" she further probed.

But the boy completely ignored her.

After a minute passed, Lynn got to her feet and started to leave.

"He hooks people," Tobias shouted at her retreating form.

Lynn straightened up and stared at him.

The boy still wouldn't look her in the eye. His gaze was intently focused on the large canvas as he continued to color in it.

But now he pressed down on the crayon so hard that the tip smeared on the paper in a thick streak of silver.

"He hooks people and they go away. But they don't just die. A person who is hooked vanishes completely, so there's no trace left of them at all. Anything they've ever owned, anything they've ever written, anything they've ever done, ALL just disappears, and no one knows that they ever existed. Not even their own parents remember them."

The boy looked up and met her eyes.

Lynn gasped and tried to comprehend exactly what he meant.

One of his eyes was ordinary brown, the other was pale blue and sightless. "So, be careful," he advised, gravely.

Lynn slowly backed away from the table. She was so distracted that she accidentally bumped into a counselor carrying a tray full of Dixie cups. On impact, several tipped and fruit punch spilled to the floor.

"Oh, I'm sorry!" Lynn apologized, blinking out of her reverie.

She stooped down to help the woman clean up the mess.

"Yeah," the woman said, rolling her eyes. "It's only the third time today."

Lynn put the fallen cups on the tray and rose to her feet. She looked at the table where the boy had been sitting.

Both Tobias and his picture were gone.

*

CHAPTER THREE
Swamp Turtles and Silver Eggs

LYNN LAID HER TOWEL fish-side-down on the sand and sat on it. The bright warm sun beat down on her and she sighed. She wasn't going to let some silly ghosts, Hookmen, or scary little boys ruin her day. It was too nice out.

She took off her tee-shirt and shorts and laid down in her bright pink one-piece suit. As soon as she hit the towel, she yelled to herself again. Forgot to bring the blasted sunscreen. With her luck, she'd turn as red as a lobster and be an even brighter shade of pink than her bathing suit.

Maybe she shouldn't lie out.

With a tired groan, Lynn sat up and surveyed the pond. Oakdale Pond's beach area was small, but the pond itself was pretty big. If she squinted hard enough, she could see the crest of trees on the other side. Unfortunately, safety buoys were set up in the deep end and no one was allowed to swim past them. Every time she went to the pond, she swam out to the buoys and hung on to them.

She would bob up and down with the light waves and stare out across the pond to the other side, wishing she was allowed to swim to it.

A few times, in a fit of rebellion, Lynn would dunk underwater and swim under the buoy, just a little bit. The lifeguard couldn't really tell if she was underwater from that distance.

Lynn frowned and glanced at the lifeguard stand. Empty. Probably because it was only early spring. It felt like a summer day, though. She was surprised more people weren't at the pond today.

There were several families: One mother was holding her baby's pudgy little arms and walking him step by baby step into the water; a teenage couple was kissing by the shore (*ew*), and three boys around her age were making mudpies and throwing them at one another.

Only four or five people were in the water.

No one was in the deep end.

She'd have that area all to herself.

Lynn got to her feet and walked to the pond. She touched her big toe to the water and shivered. It was freezing! Just the way she liked it. Lynn ran in, kicking up water on purpose to splash the kissing couple, and then dove right in.

The water was refreshing to her. It took her breath away at first, but she always got used to it after a few chilling seconds.

She rose to the surface and swam like a frog, then like a dolphin. She liked to make up her own kinds of swims because, although she was a good swimmer, she couldn't do all the technical swims so well.

But her older sister, Carly, could. When she swam she looked like a professional; pumping one arm over her head, then the other, gliding through the water like a fish. *No fair.*

Lynn tried to swim Olympic-style and got water in her mouth. She coughed, then doggy-paddled the rest of the way to the buoys in the deep end. She hung on to one of the floating white balls, which were strung together on an old frayed rope, and stared out into the pond.

She was already over her head, but yearned to swim further. She glanced over her shoulder at the people on the small beach. After all, why not? No one was looking.

Lynn took a deep breath and dove under the buoy. She swam downwards, kicking her legs like a frog.

Some leafy plants touched her face and she opened her eyes. The water was light yellowish-brown and it took her a moment to focus. The tall water plants grew from the mushy sand at the bottom and brushed against her skin as she swam downwards. She wouldn't go as far as the pond's floor. She touched the mushy sand with her foot once by accident. It felt oily and swampy. She never touched it again.

The cloud that was blocking the sun shifted and the bright rays shone down, illuminating the water in a stark, yellow glow. A glint of silver caught her eye and Lynn turned her head.

Six large silver eggs were embedded between three tall water plants. Lynn's eyes grew wide. They were so shiny, even in the murky water.

What the heck were they? By nature, she was a very curious girl and could not resist. She swam up to the eggs and laid her hand on one.

The surface of the egg felt incredibly smooth, almost like polished marble. Suddenly, she had the uncanny feeling she was being watched.

A shiver rose on the back of her neck as she slowly turned around and came face to face with a ginormous swamp turtle with glowing red eyes.

Snapping turtles were common at Oakdale Pond. It wasn't a rare event to see a large thirty-pounder crossing the street every now and then. However, Lynn had never seen a turtle bigger than herself and she most certainly never saw one with glowing red eyes.

Lynn screamed and swam out of the way as the turtle lunged forward and snapped its jaw.

She thrashed her arms and legs frantically, swimming faster than she ever swam in her life, but the large turtle was still right behind her.

Even underwater, she could hear it shrieking angrily. Then it was silent. Lynn took its silence as a sign it was opening its huge jaw to clamp down on her foot and she drew her legs up.

Sure enough, the turtle snapped its massive jaw in the very place her foot occupied moments before.

Lynn's lungs were burning. She had to get air - and fast. The turtle was shrieking behind her again. Frantically, she kicked her way up to the surface and broke through.

She inhaled a great gulp of air and started choking. She surprised a boy about her age, who was doing laps in the deep end.

"Hey," the boy called, swimming over to her. "You okay?"

Lynn's face was blue. "T-t-tur-" was all she could manage before the swamp turtle seized her right leg and dragged her underwater. It would probably feast on her once it got her to its nest. Large, black dots swam in front of her eyes and Lynn realized she was about to pass out. She fought to stay conscious, knowing if she closed her eyes now, it would be forever.

Suddenly, something was tugging on her arm. Lynn looked up and saw the brown haired, blue-eyed boy she met above the surface. The sunlight shone down on him and his blue eyes sparkled.

For a moment, Lynn was sure she was dead and she was gazing into the eyes of an angel.

The boy grabbed her hand and pulled with all his strength.

Lynn felt the turtle's grip on her leg release. It shrieked and screamed as she swam up to the surface with the boy. They broke through the water and took a huge breath.

"Oh my God," the boy shouted. "What the devil *was* that?" He turned to Lynn, who was shaking. "Come on!"

He towed her to shore. Lynn tried to help, but she felt so numb. Once they could stand, the boy propped her arm around his shoulders and he put his arm around her waist to help steady her as they walked.

The boy's friends, a black haired chubby kid, alongside a short skinny blonde boy, were still throwing mudpies at each other as they emerged from the water. The bigger kid nudged his friend and pointed at Lynn.

"Ooh, Zachys got a girlfriend!" chirped the skinny kid with mud dripping from his fingers.

"Lay off, Steve, we just got attacked," Zachary told him.

Lynn could recognize them now. The boy who rescued her was Zachary Hartman. His bigger friend was Bob Kline. The thin boy was Steven Hudson. It was a small town. She knew all their names but had never talked to them before.

They were *sixth graders*. Sixth grade boys don't talk to fifth grade girls. It wasn't considered cool. These boys were in the popular crowd too, and Lynn wasn't. She hoped they wouldn't make fun of her or anything. She didn't need that today, on top of everything else that had happened.

"Attacked?" echoed Steve, alarmed. "What, by a snapper?"

"Yeah," Zachary said. "A huge one, too!"

"Narly," commented Bob. He took Lynn's free arm as they walked her up the embankment.

"A snapper, wow," breathed Steve. "How big was it?"

"Huge," said Zachary.

"Did it have teeth?" Bob asked, expectantly.

Steve shot him a reproachful look. "Bob, how many times do I hafta tell you? Snappers ain't got no teeth. They got beaks. Sharp beaks that could break through a slab of wood in one bite. SNAAAP!" he said, demonstrating with his hands.

Lynn groaned. She sagged against Zachary and he propped her back up.

"What's wrong with her?" Steve interjected, staring at Lynn's pale face.

"She was almost lunch for a huge pond turtle, how would you feel?" Zachary snapped back.

"Oh, soooorrrry," Steve retorted, throwing his hands up in defense. "I didn't mean to hurt your girlfriend's feelings."

Zachary glared at him and he turned to Bob. "I'll take her from here."

Bob looked concerned. "Are you sure?"

"Yeah, she'll be alright," Zachary assured him.

Lynn didn't feel alright. She felt weird and lightheaded; on the verge of a panic attack. She was afraid what she would see when she looked at her leg that had been sandwiched between the swamp turtle's jaws.

Finally she forced herself to check her wound and it turned out the turtle barely scratched her. She was certain that it would have incurred more damage if Zachary hadn't come along to rescue her when he did.

"Thank you for saving me," Lynn managed breathlessly as they left the sandy beach behind and started down the path that led to the Arts and Crafts building.

"Hey, no problem," Zachary said with a smile. "I'm sure you would've done the same for me."

Lynn laughed. "I'm not sure if I could have."

Zachary's lips slowly spread into a smile and then he looked at her for a long time.

"What?" she asked. What if she had a booger or something hanging out of her nose? After all, why not? She already practically fainted on the boy today.

Zachary cleared his throat and looked down. "Your name's Lynn...*Strauss*, right?" he asked.

Lynn nodded.

"Well...uh...I was...wondering if you'd like to go out with me sometime," Zachary proposed.

Lynn was flabbergasted. *She* was being asked out on a *date*. She never went on a date before.

Carly did, once, and she said the boy smelled like a fish and complained that she didn't really have any fun.

But, Zachary was really nice.

Lynn sniffed his arm. He smelled okay.

Zachary looked amused. "What're ya doing?"

She stopped sniffing and smiled. "Yes. Let's."

His face lit up with a wide grin.

Suddenly, a white car pulled up into the lot. "Oh, that's my mom. She'll give you a ride, if you want. Where do you live?"

"Montville Manor," said Lynn.

"Hey! Me too!" He reached down and took her hand. "I live on Vermont, you?"

"New York," Lynn said, blushing furiously.

He held her hand as they walked to the car where Zachary's mother was waiting.

*

CHAPTER FOUR
The Firehouse Dance

IT WAS MONDAY. Two days had passed since Lynn had been bitten by the swamp turtle. The bell rang and it was time for recess now. She walked outside and went down the grassy hill that led to the playground.

The only people who even knew about the incident were Zachary, Bob, and Steve. Everyone else thought she just had a bike accident.

"Hey-a, Lynn!" Laurie called out from the swings. "Hurry up!"

Lynn smiled and waved at her. "I'm-a comin," she yelled back. Laurie had been a close friend of hers since second grade. She was a big girl with a loud voice. Lynn thought she was great. Devon and Andrea, her other friends from the Manor, didn't get along with Laurie as much as Lynn did.

Lynn squinted and saw Devon roll her eyes to Andrea about Laurie. Madison was there, too.

Lynn liked Maddy for the most part, but not when she acted like a know-it-all.

Madison and Andrea were in the cool crowd, more so than Laurie, Lynn, or Devon.

Andrea envied Madison and wanted to be like her. She often portrayed Maddy's parrot, echoing everything the girl said.

Lynn sat on the swing next to Madison and let out a long sigh.

"Where were you?" Maddy admonished Lynn.

"Yeah, where were you?" chimed in Andrea.

Lynn looked from one to the other. "Taking my sweet time."

"You always faking your fime," Laurie slurred with a tootsie pop in her mouth.

"What?" said Lynn.

Laurie took the pop out of her mouth with chocolate stains between her teeth. "You always take your time. You almost missed recess," she said as she plopped the pop back in her mouth and looked away.

Maddy stared at Laurie with a look of disgust, then looked away. "Ew. That is *so* gross."

"Disgusting," agreed Andrea.

When they weren't looking, Laurie stuck her chocolately tongue out at them.

Devon noticed and laughed.

Lynn surveyed her friends and found herself giving them labels. Madison: The Queen. Andrea: The Princess. Devon: The Knight. Laurie: The Joker. What was she? She tried to think up other royal titles, but nothing came to mind. Maybe she was a knight, too. After all, she didn't really care about getting her hands dirty every now and again.

The cleanest girl in the world award went to Andrea Parks. Her room was meticulous every time Lynn went to visit her. There was a place for everything and everything in its place. Even now, when they were playing on the swings at recess, Andrea was picking lint off her skirt.

"Andrea, you look fine," Lynn assured her. "I don't even see any lint on you."

"I do," Andrea said without looking up. "And I can't be one speck dirty."

"I can!" declared Laurie, laughing vehemently. She pumped her legs too fast and her lollipop slipped from her sticky fingers and it landed directly in Andrea's lap.

Andrea shrieked as if the gooey candy was a snake and kicked her legs. "Ew! Eeeeew! Get it off me! Get it off me!" she squealed.

Lynn tried not to laugh, although it was very difficult not to. She wondered how Andrea would react to a snapping turtle.

"Relax, girl. I got it," Devon told her. She picked off the lollipop with two fingers and threw it into the field.

Laurie was still laughing aloud. "Nice save, Andrea!"

Andrea's face was molten red and her eyes threatened tears. "It just better not leave a stain," she warned.

Laurie stopped laughing. She didn't want to get in trouble with Andrea's mom.

Lynn was twirling slowly around in the swing, making trails with her foot in the dirt when Madison squealed: "Look! It's Zach Hartman."

Lynn looked up and saw Zachary, Bob, and Steve on the jungle gym. They were on the top, looking over at them.

"Are they looking at us?" squeaked Andrea. Her hands flew frantically to her hair. "How's my hair?"

"Oh, it looks fine, Andrea, as usual," Devon assured her.

"Zachary who?" Laurie asked.

Maddy ran her fingers through her own curly blonde hair. "Come on, Laurie. Don't you know anything? He's Zachary Hartman, only the cutest boy in school."

"He's a sixth grade*r*," hissed Andrea.

They better lay off, Lynn thought sourly. She reached her hand up to fix her own long blonde hair, but quickly put it back down.

She didn't want to look like a girly-girl. If he didn't like her with tangly hair, then he could have Maddy or Andrea.

The boys hopped down from the jungle gym and started to walk over to the swings. Steve, the thin kid, waved.

Madison performed the Guinness Book of World Records biggest intake of breath, waving her hands frantically in front of her face. "They're coming! They're coming!"

"Hi'ya, Lynn!" Steve said, cheerfully.

"Hey," Lynn said.

She felt all the girls' stares at once.

"How's your leg?" he asked.

Please don't mention the snapper, oh please don't mention the snapper, Lynn silently begged.

"Better," she said.

Zachary went over to the empty swing next to her and sat down. He was silent for a moment, staring at her with his incredibly blue eyes, then he smiled and lightly bumped her swing with his.

"I was just, uh wondering-" his voice cut off as he cleared his throat. "if you'd like to go to the Firehouse Dance with me this Friday night."

Maddy shrieked with glee and hit Lynn's arm three times.

"Ow ow ow!" yelled Lynn. "Cut it out!" Then, she looked at Zachary and smiled. "Sure, Zachary. I'd love to go."

"Great!" Zachary said, brightening up. "Let me get your number-" He glanced around Lynn at the girls on the swings, who were staring at him in awe. "Anyone got a pen?"

They shook their heads.

Maddy batted her eyelashes.

"Here you go," Bob offered, handing Zachary a marker from his pants pocket. He winked at Andrea, who blushed and looked at the ground.

"Thanks, man," said Zachary.

He handed the marker to Lynn, then held out his hand. "I don't have a paper to write on," he said, sheepishly. "Just write it on my palm."

Lynn scribbled her number on his palm and he smiled.

"That tickles."

"Sorry," she apologized.

"Okay if my mom picks you up about seven?"

Lynn wasn't sure she was even allowed to go. Her mom never let her go out past dark, unless it was for a sleepover at a friend's house and she knew their parents.

Lynn groaned inwardly. If her mom asked to speak to Zachary's parents before they left she'd just die. "Sure, that sounds great."

"Great," Zachary said. He lightly tapped the tip of her nose with his finger. "See you then."

"Yep, see you then," Lynn said, barely able to contain her excitement.

The boys slowly walked away and her friends erupted into a squealing fit. They started talking all at once.

"How did you meet him?" asked Laurie.

"Lynn, you never told us you ever talked to him!" accused Madison.

"What're you going to wear?" asked Laurie.

"Wow, he's sooo cute!" squealed Andrea in awestruck admiration.

"So does this mean he's your boyfriend now?" questioned Laurie.

Lynn blocked out their voices and stared up at the white clouds in the blue sky. She couldn't wait for the dance.

*

Mrs. Hartman picked Lynn up at 6:45. Despite Lynn's desperate begging and pleading, her mom insisted on meeting Zachary's mother before they went anywhere.

Lynn sat in the backseat next to Zachary, blushing furiously, while the two adults talked. Zachary smiled and nudged her with his elbow.

"You look really pretty tonight," he whispered. Then, he reached down in the seat and handed her a pink rose.

"Aw, thanks," Lynn said, feeling her anxiety and embarrassment vanishing. That is, until her mother rapped on the windowpane and waved.

Zachary rolled down the window.

"I will pick up you guys at ten o'clock sharp," Lynn's mom said with a smile. "Meet me outside or I'll beep the horn."

"Okay, Ma!" Lynn called out a little too loudly.

Mrs. Hartman pulled out of the driveway and drove up New York Road, taking a left on Chapel Hill Road to get to the Firehouse. The Firehouse held a dance once a month from 7-10 p.m. This was Lynn's first time going, but she heard a lot about them from Carly, Devon, and Laurie.

They said bye to Zachary's mom and got out of the car. She drove away and Zachary took Lynn's hand in his as they went inside.

"Wow," Lynn gasped. The Firehouse was fully packed. She recognized a lot of kids from school and also saw The Manor Boys. The Manor Boys were trouble. They were a group of eighth grade bullies that tease everyone, especially girls.

Lynn led Zachary away from them to the chairs beside the refreshment table.

"What's up?" Zachary asked as he pulled out a chair for her and they sat down.

Lynn indiscreetly pointed out the bullies and their ringleader, Tyler Wahrman. "Oh, I don't like those boys," she said.

Zachary frowned and looked ready to stand up. "What, do they give you trouble?"

Lynn smiled. "Nothing I can't handle."

Then, the lights went dim and the DJ put on a slow song.

Zachary cleared his throat and scratched the back of his neck. "So uh, do you want a soda or something?"

"No, thank you," Lynn said, politely.

Carly told her it was important to be polite on a first date. She said one of the reasons she never saw her ex-boyfriend again, (aside from the fact that he smelled like a fish) was because he never bothered to hold the door open for her.

Lynn knew she didn't have to hold the doors for Zach, he did that for her, but saying 'please' and 'thank you' showed him she was equally as polite.

Laurie and her little sister, Sam, walked over.

"Hi!" Laurie yelled, her loud voice carrying across the room.

"Hey, Laurie," Lynn said. "Hi, Sam. This is Zachary."

Samantha, who was only in the third grade, giggled and stuck out her hand. "Nice to meet you, sir."

Zachary took her hand and shook it firmly. "My pleasure."

Devon saw them by the chairs and came over with Andrea. For the next two slow songs, Lynn's friends crowded around Zachary and asked him twenty million questions. Lynn worried that they were being royal pains, but Zachary was being a gentleman.

Suddenly, "Without You," by Motley Crue, Lynn's favorite band ever, came on and Lynn squirmed in her seat.

Zachary noticed and said. "Want to dance?"

"Yes I do," Lynn exploded, cutting off Laurie in mid-question. She grabbed his hand, bounded out of the chair, and they went out to the strobe-lit dance floor.

Lynn pushed past the other couples dancing and found a good spot.

Zachary was still laughing as they started to slow dance. "You don't mess around, do you?"

"It's Motley Crue!" Lynn yelled, importantly.

"Ah, I see," said Zachary. He lifted his head slightly, listening to the song.

Vince Neil's voice rang out of the speakers: "Without you in my life...I'd slowly wilt and die, but with you by my side...you're the reason I'm alive-"

— "Good song," Zachary commented. He stared at Lynn for a moment, then said, excitedly: "Pick a pocket."

Lynn had her eyes closed and was quietly singing along with Vince Neil. She opened her eyes. "Huh?"

"Right or left?" Zachary asked, indicating his jean jacket.

"Um…" Lynn contemplated, wondering what he was up to. "Right?"

Zachary pulled out a gold bracelet and smiled. "Good choice."

Lynn gasped as she stared at it.

The lights caught the chain and it sparkled, casting tiny golden gleams on their faces.

Zachary was staring at Lynn with his bright blue eyes. He leaned in close to her ear and he whispered: "I think I'm in like with you."

Lynn was silent, staring at him. It was in that moment that she realized she felt exactly the same way. "I…I think I'm in like with you, too," she said, blushing.

Zachary brushed her cheek with his thumb, then lifted her hand to place the bracelet around her wrist.

"...Only you that I hold when I'm young, only you as we grow old-" sang Vince Neil.

Lynn examined the shiny golden bracelet on her wrist and she sighed. "It's so beautiful."

"So are you," Zachary whispered. He put his hand under her chin and planted a light kiss on her cheek.

"Aw, come off it, Romeo. You're makin' me sick," drawled Tyler Wahrman with his usual smirk. Two boys stood next to him, Richard Crawford and Tim Campbell. Richard, the dumb jock, cracked his knuckles.

Zachary stood in front of Lynn. "We don't want any trouble," he said with narrowed eyes.

"Uh-huh, we do," laughed Richard, dumbly.

"Is there a problem here, boys?" asked Mr. Jones, Lynn's math teacher. He looked pointedly at Tyler.

"This little punk started with us!" Tim whined to the principal.

Mr. Jones glanced at Lynn, then at Zachary. "Did you?" asked the principal.

"No sir," Zachary said. "We were just dancing. They're bothering us."

Tyler sneered and looked ready to kill him.

Mr. Jones sighed. "Follow me, Tyler. We need to have a little chat." He led the bullies away.

Tyler spun around and seized Zachary by the jacket collar. In the dim lighting, he looked even more dangerous than usual. His dark eyes were almost black. "I'll deal with you later, punk."

Zachary was very calm. Very Clint Eastwood. "Looking forward to it, trash," he replied.

After Mr. Jones took them away, Lynn turned to Zachary. "You didn't have to do that," she said.

Zachary's jaw was tight as he watched the eighth graders being led out the door. "Yes I did."

Lynn looked down. She liked Zachary a lot, she didn't want to see him get hurt.

"Hey," Zachary said, quietly. "I'm sorry. I was just sticking up for myself. That's all."

"No, I understand," said Lynn. She put her arms on his shoulders and they started to slow dance to Warrant. "Just...be careful, okay?"

"I will," Zachary said with a warm smile. "I promise."

When the dance was over, Zachary kissed her on the cheek. Lynn stood on her tiptoes to return the kiss, but then Laurie's little sister, Samantha, pushed her into him and Lynn kissed his ear.

Lynn's face turned every shade of red before leveling off at crimson and she apologized.

He smiled then leaned in close and asked her, "What're you doing tomorrow?"

*

CHAPTER FIVE
The Frog Pond

LYNN MET ZACHARY at the frog pond at 11:00 the next morning. She brought all the equipment she needed for catching tadpoles: a small hand-held net, rubber gloves, water boots, and several jars. She always released the baby frogs after she caught them, it would've been mean to take them away from their families, but it was fun to hold them in the jars for just a few minutes.

Lynn hobbled down Connecticut Blvd. in her heavy water boots, holding all her frog-catching gear in her arms. She came up on the woods at Oregon RD. and walked down the dirt trail that led to the frog pond. Her boots plodded heavy footprints into the soft, squishy dirt. She looked back at her boot prints and they looked like they were made by a hunter or a fisherman, not by an eleven year old girl. Lynn straightened up and felt very important. Today, she was an ecologist, studying the woodland animals and the plants of the forest.

"Hey!" Zachary yelled, waving at her.

He was already down the hill at the small pond. Lynn was on the other side.

The pond was more like a huge hole in the dirt, filled with light brown water. The perimeter was so small that she didn't know if 'pond' was the right word for it.

She once timed herself on walking around the whole pond and got back to her starting point in thirteen minutes.

The hills surrounding the water were steep and she was careful to watch her footing. Zachary grinned, watching her plod her way toward him.

"You look like you've done this before!" he shouted in surprise.

When Zachary asked her at the dance if she'd like to go frog-catching with him the next day, she was quick to say yes. She didn't mention that she went all the time.

"Well, you know," Lynn breathed, carefully stepping over a jutted rock on the forest ground. "I've went a few times - whoa!" she exclaimed as she tripped on a slippery stone right next to him.

Zachary caught her by the arm so that she wouldn't fall. "You look great," he said, quietly.

Lynn rolled her light blue eyes at him, then looked up at him like he had five heads. Her long blonde hair was a tangly mess around her sweaty face and her play clothes were all rumpled. She didn't put much into appearances when she was frog hunting. Maddy and Andrea didn't go to the frog pond but, if they did, they'd probably wear dresses and makeup.

Lynn stifled a sigh, imagining a meticulous-Andrea diving her hands into the muddy dirt to pull out tadpole eggs. Not in a million years.

Zachary looked like he was waiting for her to say something.

Lynn stopped giggling. *Be polite, Lynn, be polite,* Carly's words echoed in her head. "You look great too, Zachary."

He smiled at her and took her by the hand. They squatted at the edge of the pond and set the jars in the squishy dirt. The hot sun beat down on them and glinted off the glass containers. The leaves of the massive oaks above them swayed in the light spring breeze. Lynn looked at Zachary and smiled. He was surveying the water with a look of fierce concentration on his face. He, too, seemed like he'd done this before.

"See anything?" she whispered.

"Not yet," answered Zachary. "You?"

Lynn didn't but had her gloved hands ready.

"Nope," she replied.

They were silent for a few minutes. Lynn's left leg fell asleep from squatting so long. She shifted her foot, careful not to slip and fall in the pond and get her clothes soaked.

She fell in once, when she was nine, and the muddy water was definitely over her head. Lynn estimated the hole at the center, was some fifty-feet deep.

It was probably created by the same meteor that had wiped out the dinosaurs, or so she liked to believe.

"Look!" Zachary said, pointing down.

She leaned over and saw a tadpole kicking its newly formed legs, swimming in silly frog circles. "Ooh, that's a good one!"

"Go ahead, you catch it," he offered, politely. "I'll get the next one."

Lynn's hands shot out and she quickly seized the baby frog before he knew what hit him.

Zachary's eyes were wide as he stared at her. "Whoa," he breathed.

Lynn carefully placed the squirming tadpole in the jar. She was pleased that Zachary had seen her in action. She needed a plaque created that said: Lynn Strauss ~ Fastest Frog Catcher in the East. She lightly tipped the jar into the pond to add water to it and the tadpole slid and gently bumped into the side of the glass. "Sorry, little guy," she apologized to the frog.

The frog didn't answer, but seemed pleased to be submersed in water again. He swam around the jar in roundabout frog circles.

Lynn tapped the jar with her index finger and giggled helplessly as the tadpole's legs fanned out in surprise and it stared at her through beady black eyes. Zachary tilted his head to watch the frog and smiled. "Wow, that's a really good catch, Lynn. Maybe you should keep him."

Lynn stared down at the frog. The frog, whose name, she just decided, was Herbert, stared back. "Naw. Herbert wants to stay with his family."

"Herbert?" Zachary repeated, incredulously.

Lynn turned to look at him. "Yes, his name is Herbert. Don't you poke fun at him!"

Zachary swiped the muddy ground with his finger and put a muddy smear down her cheek.

Lynn gasped and threw off her glove to grab a handful of mud. Zachary held his hands up high, "Mercy! Mercy! I surrender!"

Lynn smirked and let the mud fall between her fingers to the ground. "Thought you would."

"Oh, really?" he challenged.

Lynn knelt next to Herbert and lightly tapped the jar. "Yep," she said.

A second later, she had a big mudpie hanging from her hair. Her mouth flew open as she slowly turned to Zachary, who was on his feet and doubling over with laughter. "Okay, you asked for it, buster," she seethed. She grabbed a fistful of mud and threw it full force at him.

The mudpie smacked right into his shoulder. Suddenly, it was an all out mudpie fight. Lynn squealed and ducked as a dripping dirt patty flew over her head. "Miss-" she started to say, but a second one hit her on the side of her face.

"No, I didn't!" Zachary exclaimed, laughing hysterically.

Lynn narrowed her eyes and wiped the glob of dirt off her cheek. "Now you've done it!"

She squatted by the pond and dove her hands into the water, digging for the really gooey mud.

The sticky mud was the best kind for making mudpies because it was so hard to wash off. If she was lucky, she'd pull up a mushy bundle of tadpole eggs along with it.

That would really get him good.

A movement in the center of the watering hole caught her eye and she looked at it. Thick, filmy brown air bubbles were rising and popping noisily at the surface.

Zachary knelt beside her. "What's that?" he asked, furrowing his brow.

Lynn shrugged and stared. "It's no frog," she answered. The frogs and abundant water insects sometimes made minuscule air bubbles as they rose out of the water, but these were made by something else. Something *a lot* bigger.

Zachary and Lynn leaned forward and stared.

The water was foggy but it was obvious that something was rising to the surface.

Lynn could make out a vague outline but, no matter how hard she squinted, she still couldn't quite tell what it was. However, she didn't need her glasses to see that it was coming closer with each passing second.

"Oh, God," moaned Zachary a moment later.

Lynn turned to him. He looked like he was going to be sick. "What is it?"

Zachary's face was white. He seemed unable to talk. He stared into the pond with a horrified expression as if Death itself had come to claim them on the spot.

"Zach, what is it?!" Lynn yelled, tugging on his arm.

Zachary just pointed and she looked down. Her eyes got wide as a fleshy corpse rose to the top and floated on the surface of the water. Its white eyes were wide open and its clothes were torn. Lynn felt her blood go cold.

Thick, bulging blue veins were underneath the cadaver's translucent skin. The dead man's mouth was agape and a blackened tongue hung over its blue lips.

Then, there was a nasty sucking sound as a silver hook exploded through the corpse's chest and something yanked the body back underneath the murky water.

Lynn let out a shrill and piercing scream. She scrambled away from the pond and slammed her back against the rocky embankment behind them.

Zachary remained frozen at the water's edge.

"Zach!" she screamed. "Get away! Move!"

Zachary quickly turned to her. His face was ashen and his wide eyes were horror-stricken. He seemed to be in shock. Suddenly, a slimy hand exploded from the water and seized him by the wrist. It yanked him forward and he fell into a sitting position in the mud and slid toward the pond. "No!" he screamed, using his other hand to try to pry the skeletal fingers from his wrist, but the creature's grip was inhumanely strong.

Lynn scrambled on her hands and knees and shielded her arms around Zachary's chest from behind. She gritted her teeth and pulled him back with all her strength. "Get off of him!" she screamed, kicking the fleshy hand with her foot. Lynn pulled Zachary further from the pond and the Hookman's head emerged from the water.

Staring into his hideous face, Lynn felt like her breath had been knocked out of her, all at once. The Hookman was a swamp creature with lanky black hair and severely marred skin. In the empty pits where his eyes might once have been, oozed thick, black mud. His jaw was wide open and abnormally large. Razor-sharp, brown teeth protruded out of his bleeding black gums.

"My God," whispered Lynn as the Hookman snarled and lifted his hook hand from the water. The silver tip gleamed in the bright sunlight as he raised the sharp instrument into the air and swiftly brought it down upon Zachary's exposed arm.

Lynn acted quickly. Her right leg shot out and made direct contact with the creature's face. The Hookman released his grip on Zachary's wrist and screeched like a banshee as his head was knocked backwards at an unnatural angle. The tip of his hook scraped Zachary's skin, leaving a distinct welt down the length of his arm.

Lynn and Zachary scrambled away from the pond and fled along the slope as The Hookman leaned forward and snapped his head back onto his neck.

*

CHAPTER SIX
The Fading of Zachary

ZACHARY AND LYNN EXPLODED through the front door of Zachary's house on Vermont Drive.

"Mom! Mom!" Zachary called.

A voice answered from the kitchen: "In here, sweetie!"

They bolted down the hallway. The long gash on Zachary's arm was dripping blood all over the hardwood floors. Breathless, they leaned on the counter where Mrs. Hartman was chopping up vegetables. She looked up and smiled at them. "My, you two are filthy!"

"Mom," Zachary panted. "There was a dead body in the frog pond and the Hook-"

Mrs. Hartman blinked. "Will you be joining us for dinner, Lynn?"

Their eyes bulged; stunned in silence. "Ma!" Zachary shouted. "There was a dead body in the frog pond! The Hookman tried to kill us! He-"

"What's wrong with you two?" Mrs. Hartman asked. "What's gotten into you?"

Zachary and Lynn exchanged looks. "I don't think she can understand us," Lynn surmised.

Zachary grabbed his mother's arm and spun her around. "Look! Look at what The Hookman did to me, Mom!" Zachary screamed, holding up his bloody arm in front of her face. "He tried to drag me in the pond with him! I almost died! His hook went-"

"Did I tell you we're having meatloaf tonight," Mrs. Hartman asked with a smile. She looked down and continued cutting up vegetables. "With mashed potatoes, green beans, cucumber salad-"

As his mother went on talking about dinner, Zach turned to Lynn. "Why can't she hear us?" he asked, wide-eyed.

Lynn was watching Mrs. Hartman carefully. "Oh, she can," she said, walking up to her and grabbing another steak knife. "Okay if I help, Mrs. Hartman?" asked Lynn.

Zachary's mom looked down at her. "Oh, sure, Lynn! Just be careful, that knife is sharp. Don't want you to cut yourself, ya know."

"But only when we're *not* talking about The Hookman," Lynn finished, slicing the celery and looking at Zachary.

Zachary's mouth was wide open. "Mom?"

"Yes, dear?" Mrs. Hartman replied without looking up.

"Okay if I use the phone to call the police about the dead body in the frog pond?"

"Oh sure, but make it quick. Dinner's almost ready," she replied.

Lynn was certain that Zachary's mother only heard the first half of his question. She followed Zachary into the dining room.

He lifted the receiver and dialed 9-1-1. The phone rang once, then went dead. Zachary stared at the phone in his hand.

Lynn took it from him. "Let me try my Mom." She dialed the number and it rang.

"Hello?" her mother finally answered after the third ring.

"Hi, Mom, it's me."

"Lynn?"

"Hi, Mom, just listen carefully," Lynn took a deep breath. "There's this Hookman who tried to kill Zachary and me at the frog pond today-"

"Lynn, is everything okay?"

Lynn breathed out of the side of her mouth. "No! That's what I'm trying to tell you! The..."

"Where are you?"

"I'm at Zachary's house. We're fine now, but we were almost killed by-"

"Oh, tell Tabitha hello for me and, if you eat dinner over there, be sure to use your proper table manners, Lynn, I mean it."

Lynn shook in frustration as she slammed the receiver down. "It's no use. No one can hear us if we're talking about the Hookman."

"What do we do?" Zachary asked, quietly.

Lynn was thinking hard. No moms. No police. They were on their own. "I don't know," she said.

*

Zachary awoke Monday morning with a terrible headache. He didn't have any tests scheduled today, so he decided to tough it out. Besides, he really wanted to see Lynn.

He swung his legs off the bed and jumped into his slippers. He was halfway across the room when he stopped and looked around. Something was wrong. The lights in his bedroom were too bright and everything was sharply illuminated in a soft yellow hue.

Zachary blinked and rubbed his eyes with his fists, but he still felt like he was looking at his room through a kaleidoscope.

He walked over to the bright white door and opened it. The hallway outside the bedroom was bathed in the same eerie light.

"Mom?" Zachary called as he slowly walked down the hallway. "Dad?"

The house was silent. *They must have left for work already,* he thought as he went into the bathroom and closed the door. Then, he looked in the mirror and gasped. His own reflection was not there...

Zachary lunged out of his seat as the bell rang for recess.

"Wanna play dodgeball today, Zachary?" Bob asked as they walked out of the classroom.

Zachary wanted to but couldn't. His head was throbbing. "Nah, I'll just watch," he answered, rubbing his hand down his sweaty face.

Bob was a little bit concerned. Zachary never turned down a game of dodgeball. Watching him, he could clearly see that his friend was not well and wanted to console him.

"Maybe you should go and see the nurse," he advised.

Zachary doubted she had a cure for what he had. He'd been fading in and out all day. "No, I'll be fine," Zachary said with more conviction than he felt. Then, he gasped as the unnatural lights surrounded him again.

"O-kay, if you're sure," said Bob, who turned from him to open the front door that led outside. "But, if you change your mind, I'll walk you down to there-" he cut off and looked around. Zachary was no longer behind him.

Lynn was sitting on the jungle gym at the second row from the top. She wasn't in the mood to play with her friends today. She was too concerned about Zachary. She hadn't seen him in school all day. She was absentmindedly running her finger across the metal of the gym bar when Zachary suddenly appeared next to her.

"Lynn?" he said.

Her head snapped up quick and she gasped, nearly losing her grip on the bars. "Zach! Where on earth did you come from?" She stared at him, puzzled and surprised.

He looked like he'd been crying. Gently, she put her hand on his cold cheek. "Zachary, what's wrong?"

Briefly, he told her about the lights and how he kept disappearing from view, against his will. "The school bus drove right by me, I was marked absent, I stood up and screamed at Mrs. Sinclair when she was talking and-" he trailed off and sniffed as a tear fell down his cheek. "-she didn't even notice."

Lynn felt the blood drain from her face. "And no one knows they've ever existed at all, not even their own parents," she whispered.

"Huh?"

"Oh my God," she breathed. "We've got to do something before you get worse."

Quickly, she told Zachary about what Tobias said at the camp as he colored in a picture of The Hookman. "But," she continued. "You were only *scratched* by The Hookman. If his hook pierced all the way through your arm, you would be gone completely, according to Tobias."

"So..." Zachary began, trying to understand. "The reason I keep fading in and out is 'cuz The Hookman just *scratched* me with his hook?"

"That's right," Lynn said, feeling her eyes well up with tears.

This, she felt, was her fault. She should have told him. She should have told somebody sooner. But she knew no one would believe her about the warnings she received. She hadn't even been sure she believed them herself.

Lynn told him everything then on the jungle gym under the hot spring sun. "So The Hookman was only after me...but instead, he got you," she concluded, crying uncontrollably.

She didn't bother trying to keep the tears at bay. The heck with Clint Eastwood. He never had to deal with a vicious swamp thing who hooked people and made them disappear.

Zachary put his arm around her and she cried into his shoulder. "Oh, it's okay, Lynn," he said, quietly. "None of this is your fault."

He looked up and stared into the trees behind the playground. The bright lights were bleeding through the branches.

He closed his eyes and started to fade even more into himself.

Lynn looked at him. Tears coursed down her cheeks. "I think I love you, Zachary."

And then Zachary vanished. By the way she was looking around, he could tell she no longer saw him. He lifted his hand to her cheek to wipe away a tear and she closed her eyes at his touch. "I love you too," he whispered back, but all Lynn could hear was a distant echo in her mind that made her question if she was making it up.

She smiled through her tears and opened her eyes. "Stay with me today, okay?"

"Who're you talking to?" questioned Maddy, who was standing below the jungle gym with her hands on her hips.

Lynn pursed her lips at her, wiping the tears off her face. "No one," Lynn said, climbing down the jungle gym.

"Hmm," Madison said, suspiciously.

Suddenly, Lynn had an idea. "Heya, Maddy," she started, as they walked together toward the swing sets. "Do you still do seances and stuff?"

Maddy, in addition to being a big know-it-all, was also a self-proclaimed conjurer of the dead.

Madison seemed very pleased that the subject was brought up.

"Why, of course," she answered, importantly. "I just contacted Jim Morrison last week."

"Great," Lynn said. "Listen, I need advice for a…uh, spiritual friend of mine. Someone I know is in trouble with a uh…'not-quite-of-this-world creature,'" she finished, lamely.

Madison just stared at her blankly. For one dreadful moment, Lynn was afraid she hadn't heard a word she had said. But then Miss Perfect cleared her throat, and sat down on the swing.

"Well, for advice or information in spiritual matters, you would need to talk to the farmhouse witches."

Lynn blinked and sat on the swing next to her. "The who?"

Madison shook her head and her wavy curls bounced. "Honestly, Lynn, you can be just as bad as Laurie sometimes. Don't you know anything about the Montville legends?"

Lynn certainly knew of one, off hand. "No, I guess I don't," she answered. "Who are they?"

Madison pointed to the old farmhouse in the fields behind the school playground. "Well, that's where they were."

Lynn squinted into the fields, wishing she'd brought her glasses along. "I thought that house burned down years ago and became abandoned."

63

Madison nodded. "Yep, it did burn. Over sixty years ago," she affirmed. "With the witches still inside it."

Lynn was silent. "So...they're dead witches."

Madison sighed and shook her head again as if Lynn was the dumbest person she ever had the unfortunate experience to acquaint with. "What do you think?"

"Hmm..." Lynn considered, squinting at the remains of the farmhouse.

"They're really helpful," Madison assured her. "And they've helped me out of some sticky ghost situations before. One time, this ghost Raymond used to follow me around everywhere and-"

"Will you come along with me?" Lynn asked, cutting her off. "I'm going tonight."

"Maybe," Maddy considered, then her pretty expression twisted into a look of disappointment. "Oh darn! I can't. I have cheerleading practice."

In addition to wanting to be a witch when she grew up, Madison also had aspirations of being a New England Patriots cheerleader.

"Be sure to let me know how it goes, okay?" Madison asked, lightly kicking her legs to pump the swing.

Lynn also started swinging lightly. The empty swing next to her glided over and lightly bumped into hers. She then skidded to a sudden halt and listened carefully.

"Hmmm. A little kooky, that one," Zachary's voice whispered in her ear, regarding Madison.

Lynn giggled and hushed him.

In the air, Madison looked down and frowned at the empty swing next to Lynn, which slowly glided back to its rightful place.

*

CHAPTER SEVEN
The Farmhouse Witches

LYNN AND ZACHARY WALKED up the long asphalt drive that led to the Oakdale Elementary School. They passed some apartments on the left side of the road and crossed the street to the parking lot. It was just after eleven...

Lynn felt guilty, but she had to sneak out of her house after everyone else fell asleep without telling them where she was going.

An invisible Zachary walked right beside her. She could just barely hear his footsteps echoing hers on the damp pavement.

"I keep on thinking," Zachary shouted so that Lynn could hear him. "What if one time I don't fade back to life? What if I'm forever doomed to wander around as a ghost for all eternity?"

To Lynn, it sounded like Zachary was just whispering. "You, Zachary" she said, resolutely, "are not a ghost."

Zachary was silent. "Okay, wandering spirit, then. Whichever."

Lynn smiled and turned toward the sound of his voice. "Don't worry. If Madison is right, the witches will know what to do."

Zachary was in a pessimistic mood. "What if there is no-" his voice trailed off as they reached the crest of the grassy hill to the playground. In the fields, a soft orange pulsing shone from the cracked windows of the rustic cabin.

"Ah-ha. Looks like the witches are home."

The strange lights that only Zachary could see started to dissipate. "Oh! Lynn! I think I'm-" The lights returned and he vanished again from sight. "Never mind," he said sourly.

Lynn was worried. As the day progressed, his time visible was becoming more infrequent than his time invisible. She could only guess where his shoulder was and patted it, reassuringly. "You're going to be alright," she soothed, inadvertently swatting his ear.

Zachary took her hand and they walked down the long hill. As they got closer to the witches' cabin, Lynn had a distinct feeling of uneasiness. What if Madison was fibbing about talking to the witches? Or what if they couldn't help Zachary? What if the witches were crazy?

They walked up the steps and Lynn knocked on the wooden door. She immediately wished she hadn't. It was opened by a most hideous creature second only to The Hookman.

"Ahhh!" hissed the hunched over, disgusting lump of a woman in the doorway. "A visitor!" She ushered Lynn inside, slamming the door behind her. "Blott! Mincy! Come, see, we have a visitor!" she croaked, merrily.

Something hopped into the room and Lynn gasped in revulsion. The frog woman squatted before her and stared at her through beady black eyes. Her skin was all covered in scales and boils. "'Allo!" she said in a British accent. "I'm Mincy!"

Lynn felt completely out of her realm and said nothing in return.

The brunette who opened the door had webs embedded in her hair. "My name's Plick, deary. And you are?"

Mincy gazed at Plick's hair from her squatting position on the floor and suddenly looked excited. Her bug eyes got wide and an abnormally long black tongue lashed out of her thin mouth and seized the fly that was stuck in Plick's long brown tangles.

Plick looked down at her. "Thanks for that."

"Don't mention it," Mincy cackled, chewing happily. A piece of fly fell out of her mouth and Lynn gagged in repulse.

Plick turned her head and smiled sweetly, displaying a putrid case of decayed teeth. "And what's your name, missy?"

"Lynn," she answered, nervously.

"Kindly state your business, Lynn," spoke a commanding voice from the hallway. Leaning against the door frame was a beautiful woman with long blonde hair.

"That there is Blott," Plick clarified to her.

"We need your help," Lynn said, feeling a bit relieved to see a normal person.

"We?" Blott asked, raising a perfectly arched eyebrow. She moved through the room. Her long red dress gracefully swayed around her flawless figure. "Who is we, dear?"

"Me and Zachary," Lynn said, pointing to the empty space adjacent to her. "Well, he's invisible because-"

"Ah-ha, why an invisible friend," mused Blott, critically evaluating the empty space beside Lynn with her bright green eyes. "How *intriguing*."

Lynn's gaze swept the room. It was every bit a witches' cabin, complete with a steaming black cauldron in the center of the room.

Masses of spiderwebs hung down from the rotten beams that held together what was left of the chipped and cracked ceiling.

Amber-colored jars lined rusty shelves along the far side wall, and they were filled to the brim with insects, body parts, and other things that Lynn couldn't identify. There, a pair of blue eyes stared out at her from one of the smaller jars and her mouth flew open as one of the eyes winked, conspiratorially.

The frog-witch cackled, delighted with Lynn's reaction to the floating eyeballs. "I caught that bloke meself at Haughton Cove. 'Andsome little devil, isn't 'e?"

Blott rolled her eyes and fluttered away in a flourish of red satin. "Have a seat," she offered.

Lynn protested in surprise as two old wooden chairs fell from the ceiling behind her. The chair scooped her off the ground, then leaned back so her feet no longer touched the floor. The chair glided forward on its two legs, guided by Blott's upraised finger.

"Now," Blott intoned, lowering her finger to halt the chairs and lower the legs to the floor. "I gather you want information or advice of some kind, am I right?" she asked, her voice as cold as a winter rain.

"Yes," Lynn answered, gratefully. "We need to know-"

"Well," Blott interrupted, "Plick is the expert of such knowledge, aren't you, Plick?" she probed. Plink, however, didn't seem like she wanted to be bothered with such trivialities.

"Ah, yes, Blott, I suppose," Plick affirmed.

She crossed in front of Lynn and blocked out the view of Blott, who seemed to be busy mixing a mysterious concoction in a large silver bowl at the table with her back turned to them.

"We do specialize in information of all kinds: directions, questions, inquiries, riddles, puzzles, mazes, and maps of the underworld-"

"No," Lynn interrupted. "All we really need to know is how to cure someone who's been hooked by the Legend they call The Hookman."

Blott's stirring spoon clanged against the side of the bowl.

Lynn sat there, gauging their reactions.

Plick let out a raspy cackle. "There's no curing Death, missus."

Lynn inclined her head toward the empty seat next to her. "Zachary's not dead."

Mincy leaned forward and let out a loud gasp. "Could it be? Blott, could he be the one?"

"Hush your tongue!" Blott screamed out. Her serene expression was gone and her face twisted in anger as she swung her pale hand back and slapped Mincy hard in the face. Several new boils instantly formed on the frog woman's cheek that was already plagued with enough.

"A few more slip-ups, Mince; a *precious* few more, I warn you - you'll spend the rest of your days croaking in a pond!"

Plick scowled, turning her attention toward Blott. "Is it ready?'

Lynn's eyes widened as Blott handed Plick a silver bowl. "What is that?" asked Lynn.

Plick put her wrinkled hand into the bowl and drew out a pile of white powder.

"Un-disappearing dust," she mumbled. She sprinkled it on the empty seat and Zachary, who was coughing, slowly faded into view.

"Zach!" Lynn exclaimed, happily.

"Geez, it smells bad," he complained, trying to brush the powder off his face.

Plick put her gnarled finger under Zachary's chin, narrowed her eyes, and closely examined his face. "Hmm," she considered. "You should be dead."

"But he isn't," pointed out Lynn. "What can we do to help him?"

Plick stood tiptoed and quickly glided across the room to stand directly in front of Lynn, who felt a strange jolt as the witch's mud brown eyes bore into hers. It was as if the strange woman was probing into her soul.

Lynn, who felt very uncomfortable with this arrangement, quickly looked away. After a long pause, the witch croaked.

"Now whatever would the great and powerful Hookman want with such a scrawny, loathsome creature like yourself?"

Lynn sniffed. "Speak for yourself, ma'am" she mumbled.

The witch sneered and stepped away.

Patience was not quite one of Lynn's stronger qualities. She stamped her foot on the ground. "So can you help us or not?"

"Oh, yesss, we can help you," Blott crowed. "But, before we can tell you anything, we will be requiring something from you…"

Please don't say my soul, please don't say my soul, Lynn silently begged.

Blott stared at Lynn's long golden locks and lightly ran her fingers through it. "Over time," she began, softly. "Our good looks fade and we'll start to wither." She placed her fingers under Lynn's wrist and gently elevated Lynn's hand to examine her fingernails. "We need a fresh supply of healthy…*parts* to maintain our beauty-"

For some reason Lynn thought of Madison.

"Otherwise," the beautiful witch continued, "we'll start to look like *this.*"

Her flawless skin peeled away from her bones as fleshy layers transformed into an ugliness that rivaled The Hookman's.

Lynn screamed and closed her eyes. She felt the witch's gory hand press against her skin as Blott squeezed her fingers together.

The witch's flesh dripped down Lynn's hand and landed in a gooey heap on the floor.

"Holy Jesus," Zachary breathed, staring at the slimy creature in horror.

"We can't have that happen now, can we?" the witch asked in a croaking voice.

"No, God, no!" affirmed Lynn.

"Good," Blott said, most satisfied. She drew in a deep breath and the loose skin reformed on her face and arms. "I'm so glad that we've come to an understanding."

Lynn's eyes flew open. The witch was back to normal in appearance.

Blott smirked and released her wrist.

As quick as a flash of lightning, she seized a pair of scissors from the table and circled around Lynn, roughly yanking her hair back.

"Ow!" Lynn yelled as her neck slammed into the back of the chair.

"Stop!" screamed Zachary. He pushed back the chair and jumped to his feet.

Blott's green eyes flashed violet and he was shoved back into his seat without her touching him. Then, her strange eyes focused on Lynn.

"You want information. I want hair. What's it going to be?" bargained the witch.

"Take it! Please, take it!" Lynn screamed. The witch was pulling on it so hard she was surprised it hadn't been yanked out already.

"Lynn, no!" begged Zachary.

"Zachary, for God's sake, it's only hair, it will grow back!" Lynn snarled through clenched teeth. Besides, given this witch's manner, she was sure it would be taken regardless of her answer.

Blott smiled and chopped the shears close to her neckline. Lynn watched the golden pieces fall to the floor at her feet. *Oh, well*, she mourned.

When the cruel witch was finished, she held up the long strands, which shined of gold in the candlelight. "Ahh, that's beautiful," she breathed and released Lynn.

Lynn sat up and ran her fingers through her hair. It felt choppy and really short.

"Be glad that I left you with something," Blott remarked. She started to cackle hideously again. The other witches joined in and the small cabin was filled with a cacophony of screeching uproar.

Zachary leaned over. "Do ya think they would melt if we poured water on them?" he whispered to Lynn.

Then suddenly the witches' laughter abruptly ceased and they stared at Zachary.

Zachary sat back in his seat. "I'm sorry," he quickly apologized.

Plick stepped closer to them. "Now, you shall receive the knowledge we promised to you."

She leaned against the table, closed her eyes, and raised her arms skyward. "The ever powerful, all knowing Hookman of-"

" 'E's so 'andsome!" interrupted Mincy.

Blott's eyes glowed green as she slapped her across the face.

Mincy's wail was so horrible that Zachary and Lynn had to cover their ears.

Plick rolled her eyes and looked bored as she recited the incantation:

Poor Mincy howled as she fell onto the floor;
Shed her green skin and crawled for the door.
Her nails, they broke off, brittle as they tore.
Where once there was a woman one before...
There now lies a witch-like old hag no more.

Lynn's eyes widened as the bloated, croaking frog hopped out of Mincy's old rags. It squeezed under the crack in the front door and was lost to the night.

"Pity," Blott said, unconcerned. "There goes another one of our kind."

"Another one?" Zachary asked, all wide-eyed and in disbelief.

"Well, yes," Blott stated. "Honestly, dear boy. Where do you suppose all those frogs come from at your beloved frog pond?"

Lynn was sure if she had a mirror, her face would be as green as Mincy's.

"Oh, that's gross," she whispered, feeling sick.

"On with it already, Plick," Blott said with a swift wave of her hand.

*

CHAPTER EIGHT
Indian Myths and Curses

"FOR THOUSANDS OF YEARS," explained Plick, "an ancient Indian tribe inhabited the area which is now known as Montville, CT. Two hundred years ago a fierce group of settlers arrived, led by their bloodthirsty captain. This captain waged war on the peaceful Indians, trying to drive them from their own land. The Indian chief refused to leave. In retaliation, the white captain killed the Indian chief's young twin daughters and posted their decapitated heads on totem poles in front of the campgrounds. The captain did this not only in revenge, but to also serve as a warning: *leave this land or die.* What he did not know was that the chief was skilled in the Ways of the Other World.

The chief of the tribe, fueled by his anger and driven by his hatred for the man responsible for the untimely deaths of his only two daughters, grew more powerful and set upon the captain a terrible curse. He later cut off the captain's hand and recited the Infliction...

Ever since, the captain was to forever roam the world as a creature not alive or dead, but damned. The men of the captain's crew were also cursed to remain on this earth in spiritual limbo. They are doomed to dwell forever in the forests of the Oxoboxo River, the very same area where they captured the chief's daughters years upon years ago."

Plick's voice had a certain hypnotizing quality to it as Lynn listened to her rhythmic speech with her eyes closed.

Once Plick had finished telling the ancient story, Blott smiled warmly and added, "...It only seems like only yesterday, doesn't it?"

"Indeed it does," Plick replied with a regretful sigh, as if that had been the best time of her life.

"So," began Lynn, trying to understand. "the Indian chief turned the captain into a Hookman after he killed his little girls?"

The witches smiled gleefully.

"Absolutely dreadful, isn't it, my child?" Plick exclaimed. They burst into another fit of witchy, almost drunken laughter.

"Yes it is," Lynn said with a frown. "Why have we never heard about this in our history books?"

The witches stopped laughing and turned to Lynn. "Well, all records pertaining to the captain and his crew were burned. There are no records of their existence at all," Plick stated.

"So, that's why he erases people?" Lynn spat out, angrily. "Because he was erased?"

The witches exchanged looks.

"Well, that's part of it, yes," Plick said.

Lynn crossed her arms. "Well he deserves the curse he got!"

Blott snarled and lifted her hand high in the air to slap her when Plick squealed: "Look!"

"What?" Blott snapped impatiently with her hand poised over Lynn's face.

Plick was busy gazing at Zach. "He has The Mark upon him!" she gasped.

Zachary blinked in surprise and searched his body for marks. Baffled, he turned to Lynn, who shrugged her shoulders.

"Well," Blott replied, lowering her hand and turning to Lynn with a satisfied smirk, "as fate would have it, The Hookman's curse will soon be lifted. He has chosen his Successor."

Lynn's eyes got wide.

Zachary was equally as baffled.

"Oh, that doesn't sound good at all," Zachary said nervously.

"A successor? What exactly do you mean?" chimed in Lynn.

Blott rolled her eyes. "The Hookman has been searching for a worthy replacement for years. He grows weary of-"

"You mean The Hookman wants to *retire*?" Lynn asked, stunned.

Zachary gasped. "Well, I won't do it!"

Plick cackled softly and rubbed at the wart on her nose. "Well, you won't have much of a choice in the matter, I'm afraid."

"Wait a minute," interjected Lynn. "How can The Hookman pass his curse to someone else?"

Blott let out a sigh as if she never heard such a stupid question before. "Over the decades, The Hookman has skilled himself in the Ways of the Other World. He knows how to perform the same ritual that was afflicted upon him." She narrowed her eyes and shot Zachary a cursory glance. "You, my boy, will become the next Hookman, whether you want to or not - and we will serve you well in return ."

Not if I can help it, Lynn thought, resolutely.

Zachary looked from Blott to the wall behind her. Oscillating beneath the wooden surface were the multicolored lights. He closed his eyes as the brilliance engulfed him and he disappeared from plain view.

Blott and Plick gasped, as they moved as one like an orchestrated pair of Siamese twins.

"The powder, Plick!" Blott screamed as she lunged forward. "Get the powder! "

Plick hobbled over to the table and, in her frantic rush, tripped over a small stool and fell to the floor with a loud thud.

Blott's hands frantically searched the entire area that Zachary had occupied moments before. Her features contorted to an expression of rage. "Where are you, you wretched boy!"

Everyone froze and stared as the front door opened by an invisible force and then slammed shut.

Blott slammed her fist on the table. "You let him get away!"

Plick was huddled in a corner, clutching the silver bowl in her trembling hands. "I-I'm sorry, Blott," she apologized. "You know, The Hookman will be able to find him wherever he hides."

Blott sighed, regretfully, and brushed her hair out of her face. "I would have liked to have been the one to deliver him," she lashed out. Her eyes flashed and she turned to Lynn. "Come on," she hissed, vehemently. She seized Lynn by the arm and lifted her from the seat.

"Where are we going?" asked Lynn.

"Shut up!"

Blott led her down the hallway to a wooden door, with Plick following closely at their heels.

Lynn surveyed the old door and gasped.

The gargoyle carvings on the frame were alive and moving. One of the small wooden creatures looked at her through its bright red eyes and let out a muffled growl.

She struggled to free herself from the witch's firm grip. "Let me go! Let me go! " she screamed in protest.

Blott's lips curled into a sneer and she opened the door. Down the small flight of stairs was a basement with earthen floors.

Blott pulled Lynn close to her and whispered menacingly in her ear: "Listen, you've caused me enough aggravation today, little one." And then violently, she shoved her down the stairs.

Lynn landed hard on the filthy dirt floor and winced as a dust cloud formed around her face. The witches loomed there in the doorway with a silhouette of light permeating from the flaming torches that aligned the circular room.

Blott's voice was low as she crossed her arms in an "X" in front of her, thrust them forward in a quick gesture, then said: "Hex."

Lynn tilted her head up, feeling disorientated and confused.

Plick cackled merrily and held up the long strands of Lynn's hair that she clutched in her withered hands. "That means you're jinxed from this day forth. We still have your hair!"

Lynn pouted as she crossed her arms around her chest and the witches squealed gleefully then slammed the door behind them.

Lynn was left alone in the silent, dirt-floored room. She walked to the center of the cavern, sat down, and hugged her arms around her knees.

Suddenly, Zachary appeared beside her and laid his hand on her arm. "Hey-" he whispered.

Lynn jumped up in surprise and slapped him across the face. "Oh, Zach, I'm sorry!" she cried, mortified. "I didn't know it was you."

Zachary held his hand to his red cheek. "It's okay," he said, winking at her. "Serves me right for sneaking up on you all the time."

Lynn giggled. They were silent for a moment.

"Oh, Zach, why didn't you try to escape?" she admonished, gently.

Zachary raised an eyebrow at her. "And leave behind a damsel in distress. Nev-a!" he declared in a knightly voice.

"No, seriously," insisted Lynn. "You should've gotten out while you had the chance."

Zachary put his arm around her shoulders. "I'd never leave you behind," he said, softly.

Lynn rested her head upon his shoulder. "So, how do you suppose we'll get out of here?" she asked, then frowned. "What's that?"

Leaning against the muddy wall across from where they sat was a red velvet holder. Zachary stood and crossed the room to stare down at it.

"I don't know," he said, cautiously lifting the long case from the dirt floor and undoing the red ribbon that was tied around it. The ribbon fell to the ground and Zachary reached in the case. His hand enclosed around cold metal and he slowly unsheathed a long, golden sword.

The gold reflected in the light of the flaming torches and Lynn let out a gasp. "Oh, wow," she said, impressed.

"Look. There's an inscription on the handle," Zachary pointed out, holding the golden sword up to the light. "It's some kind of riddle..."

A dreaded beast from the Days of Old-
Impossible to slay me; as the Story is told.
I have nine heads and a body of scale-
Which you shall see if you should fail.
Many have perished at the fire of my breath.
One hit of my venom will bring you to death.
For now, I will give you just one last clue-
The fiery, murky swamps is where I grew.
WHO AM I?"

Zachary and Lynn stared at each other.

"Usually, in mythology, if you couldn't solve a riddle within a certain time frame you would find out the answer the hard way," Zachary whispered with nervous uncertainty.

Lynn's brow was furrowed in concentration. "Oh wait, what's the name of that thing with the heads..." she said, snapping her fingers. "Darn! I should have paid more attention in mythology class last month."

"Ooh! Wait I know! It's a Hy..." she trailed off, staring at the creature that emerged out of the wall behind Zachary. "Hydra," she whispered.

The beast that loomed over them was a scaly serpent with nine heads and nine hissing mouths. Each serpent displayed rows of gleaming, razor-sharp fangs and mouths of fire. Lynn and Zach slowly backed away from the creature.

Within the walls of the earthen basement was an awful groaning sound as the wood stretched and the room expanded to accommodate the for the snake-monster's immense size.

Lynn dared to look away for a brief moment and watched in awe as the ceiling receded from view. Then she locked eyes on the Hydra.

"Zach, look out!" screamed Lynn as the snake lunged forward. Zachary took a step back just in time and swung the golden sword at the beast's neck. The amazingly sharp blade pierced straight through its scales. One of the snake's decapitated heads fell to the floor in a bloody heap.

"One down, eight to go!" Zachary announced. He stared at the open wound in horror. "Oh no," he whispered. Two heads regenerated and grew in place of the head he just severed.

"Zach!" Lynn yelled. She threw herself to the ground as one of the snakes swooped down upon them. They felt its massive body swish over them.

Zachary jumped aside, madly swinging the golden sword.

"What do we do?" Lynn screamed.

"Catch!" Zachary threw the sword and Lynn caught it with one hand.

The serpent hissed. Its eyes glowed furiously and spittle poured from the corner of its mouth, dripping in wisps of flames.

Lynn slashed and plunged the sword down through its neck. A terrible screeching erupted from the creature. "Zach! Here!" she yelled and tossed the sword back to him.

Something was reforming in the open gash in front of her. Lynn reached up and grabbed a flaming torch from the wall and waited. The baby snake heads writhed in the open wound, waiting to grow enough to lash out at her.

Lynn tilted her head and watched them. The baby snakes couldn't even open their eyes yet. For the moment, they were defenseless. Carefully, she pressed the flaming torch down into the open wound and the blood immediately turned black.

The baby snakes hissed and squirmed, then fell to the ground in two piles of ash at her feet. No recurring heads grew. She let out a breath of delight and ran to Zachary, who was swinging at a snake head across the room.

"I can't do it," he panted. "They just keep on growing back."

"You have to burn them with a torch!" Lynn yelled.

Zachary raised the sword into the air above the point where all the heads were connected. "Lynn, are you sure?" he asked, breathlessly.

"Positive!"

Zachary had to chop the sword down three times in order to cut through all the scaly layers. The Hydra's wail was the most dreadful sound Lynn had ever heard. She wanted to crouch down and cover her ears, but she knew she had to hold the torch ready.

The fifteen heads lay dead on the dirt floor. Instantly, thirty new ones began to form within the bloody mass of what remained of the Hydra and its mutating offspring.

Lynn then drove the torch deep into the hole. Instantly, the skin started to blacken.

"Whoa, it works!" exclaimed Zachary. He set the torch down to the other side, which shriveled immediately.

Once the entire mass was dead and no longer recoiling, they set the torches back into the wall and silently watched the monster melt to death. A large glob of pus oozed out right next to Lynn's sneaker.

"Wanna roast some marshmallows?" Zachary suggested.

Lynn turned to Zachary; her expression grim. "Ew. That's so gross," she stated, sounding much like Madison would under similar circumstances.

They started laughing and hugged each other.

Zachary pulled away first and smiled as he studied Lynn.

"You know. Your hair looks kinda cute short. It actually suits you. Very warrior-like. Tres de Joan of Arc."

Lynn laughed and shoved him away. "Stop it. You're teasing me."

"No, I mean it," Zachary laughed, holding his hands up in a defensive gesture. "And the green goo all over your sneakers really brings out the color of your eyes."

"Oh, hush, you!" she scolded. They heard a scraping noise across the floor above their heads. "Oh yeah. Crazy killer witches upstairs. We gotta jet," Lynn warned.

She led him to the wall where she'd first seen the Hydra appear. The wall seemed solid. "Here's hoping we get out," she said, crossing her fingers.

They closed their eyes, held their breaths, and stepped right through the muddy wall.

Lynn felt dirt all around her and she pushed her way through about ten feet of loose soil.

Soon she felt a breeze on her fingertips and, a moment later, she was free from the soil and she emerged into a hollowed dirt tunnel that led to the land above.

Zachary stepped out of the wall and brushed himself off as he stood next to her and looked up. They stared up at the stars in the clear night sky as they held hands and continued up the tunnel.

Zachary crawled out first, reaching his hands down to pull Lynn to ground level. She scanned the surrounding area.

They found themselves in the woods behind the soccer field, right near the portables of their elementary school.

Zachary helped brush the dirt off Lynn's back. "Well," he teased. "We'll have to thank Madison. Her witches were most courteous and kind."

Lynn was silent and Zachary looked at her. A large tear spilled from her eye and glimmered on her cheek.

"Hey, what's wrong?" he asked.

"I'm so sorry. For everything," she replied.

Zachary reached his arms out and she hugged him. "It's all going to be okay," he assured her, running his hand down her hair. "I just have to stay away from The Hookman. That's all. Okay? It's going to be alright."

Lynn pulled away and said, "Yeah. Okay."

"Hey," Zachary soothed, studying her. "You're not thinking of contacting anyone else for help, are you?"

"Nah," Lynn lied.

"Good. We don't need another incident like the one we had tonight," he said with a grin.

He took her by the hand and they walked out of the forest and onto the soccer field.

Lynn returned his smile and looked up at the dimly lit street that was ahead of them, beyond the fields.

The best way to get to the bear is through its cubs, she thought. And the best way to stick it to The Hookman is to have a little chat with his old crew...

*

CHAPTER NINE
The Oxoboxo River Ghosts

LYNN WAS TAKING A BOWL out of the cupboard for her frosted flakes when the phone rang.

"I'll get it!" exclaimed Carly, who bounded into the kitchen, wearing her tight green spandex pants and a white workout tank top.

All morning long, she had been in the living room, practicing her routine for the talent show next week. The Beach Boys "Aruba" blared out of the speakers.

"*I'll* get it," her mother corrected.

Carly huffed melodramatically and spun on her heel. She stopped in her tracks and did a quick double-take. "Wow, Lynn, what happened to your hair?"

Lynn shrugged and sat down at the table. "I cut it off."

"It looks nice," their mother said, giving Carly The Look.

"It looks very short," Carly remarked, circling around her younger sister to examine her hair.

Lynn's mother quickly wiped her hands on a dishtowel before picking up the phone. "Hello?"

"So, you butchered it yourself?" asked Carly, going into the fridge to get her water bottle.

"Yes, I did," Lynn answered, proudly.

Carly raised her eyebrows and put the bottle to her lips. "Nice hack job."

"Thank you," replied Lynn with a curt nod.

"Yes, she's here," her mom was saying. "Hold on." She cupped her hand on the receiver. "Lynn, it's Zachary."

Lynn quickly wiped her mouth on her napkin and got up from the chair.

"Ooo, Lynnie's got a little boyfriend," chimed Carly in a taunting tone.

Lynn spun around to face her. "Well at least he doesn't smell like Mystic Seaport," she jabbed with a wicked grin.

Carly opened up her mouth to say something, but then shut it. Instead, she sighed and mushed her cornflakes against the side of her breakfast bowl with her spoon.

"Is he okay?" Lynn's mom asked, concerned.

Lynn firmly cupped the phone with her hand as her mother walked away. "Zach?"

"Hey," Zachary said in a weak voice.

"Oh yesss, you're a cute little bud," her mom said in the background. Lynn turned around and saw that her mother was watering the plants in the windowsill.

She always told Lynn and Carly that talking to plants helps them to grow, and that's just what she was doing right now. "Here's another drink for you so you can get big and strong. Ooh! We are thirsty today, aren't we? You sweet, tiny-"

As her mom went on, Carly watched her with big, scared eyes.

"Mom!" shouted Lynn, silencing her.

Her mother looked up briefly and shrugged, then lowered her voice and whispered into the leaves of the plant: "No respect at all."

"Zach," Lynn said, her attention returning to the phone. "Are you okay?"

Zachary sighed and was silent.

"What's wrong?"

"I'm really sick, Lynn."

Lynn froze mid-pace. "How sick?"

"Well, I'm better, now that I'm in the house," Zachary confided. "But, as soon as I went outside, it felt like-" he trailed off.

"Like what?" Lynn asked, fearfully.

"It felt like the sunlight was killing me."

Lynn was silent. Then, she said: "I'm coming right over."

"No Lynn," he insisted. "Go to school. I'm just going to sleep in all day anyway." He managed a weak laugh. "You'd be bored."

"No, I won't," stated Lynn. "I'm on my way."

"Lynn, really. You'll get in trouble."

"Since when has that ever stopped me from doing anything?"

Zachary laughed, but then was besieged by a coughing fit.

"Oh, Zachary, what can I do?" Lynn asked, feeling completely helpless. He was still coughing; unable to answer her. She felt her eyes tearing up. He sounded really bad.

"Zach, you can't be alone."

"Yes I can," he replied once his voice returned. After a long, silent moment, he conceded. "If you really want to come see me, come by after school. But I'm warning you now ahead of time, it's not a pretty sight."

"Okay," Lynn sniffed.

"Okay."

"See you soon," she said. "Just stay inside your house until I get there."

"I will."

"Bye," said Lynn.

"Bye," said Zachary.

After she hung up the phone, she quickly left the room and went upstairs before her mom or Carly could see the tears in her eyes.

She started to walk into her room when she heard an inquisitive "gah?" from the pink room across the hallway.

Lynn poked her head into her baby sister's room. Jessica was standing in her crib, holding the bars, and rocking back and forth. Her face brightened into a huge baby smile when she saw Lynn appear.

"Eee!" Jessie exclaimed. In her excitement, she fell over backwards and landed on her diaper.

Lynn walked over to the crib and lifted her up. "You're such a silly baby," she said, bobbing her up and down.

"Neeeeee-oh!" Jessie yelled happily, swatting her little hand on Lynn's cheek.

And like most two year olds, Jessica's favorite word was "no."

Lynn sat on the floor with her little sister in her arms. "Jessie, can I tell you something?"

Jessica stared up at her with large wide eyes and made an 'O' mouth.

"You're the only person I can talk to about this," Lynn said. "Everybody else would think I was crazy."

"Gee!" exclaimed Jessie.

"Me and Zachary are in *big* trouble," Lynn confided. "The Hookman has-"

"Oookan!" yelled Jessie.

Lynn quickly looked at her. "You heard me say Hookman?"

"Oookaaan!" Jessica repeated, exuberantly.

Lynn became silent. How could her little baby sister hear her say 'Hookman,' but no one else? She frowned and thought it over. It must be that only adults couldn't hear about "The Hookman." He didn't see children as a threat to him! Lynn thought about Zachary and his terrible curse and her eyes welled up in tears.

"Ug." Jessica offered, holding her little arms out to Lynn, sensing her distress.

Lynn wrapped her arms around her tiny baby sister's head and started to cry.

After enough time had passed, Jessica started to squirm and grunt, trying to get free. "Neee-oh. Neee-oh!" she complained.

Suddenly, there was a ripping scream coming from downstairs.

Lynn's head snapped up and her eyes grew wide.

Her mother was screaming hysterically. "Get off him! Get off him!"

Lynn's heart started pounding heavily in her chest. He got her father. The Hookman was here. "Hide, Jessie, hide quick!" she urged, frantically.

Hide and seek was Jessica's favorite game. She squealed with delight and hobbled across the room.

Lynn ran out of the room and bolted down the stairs. "Dad! Daddy!" In her frantic rush, she slipped and fell down the last five stairs.

She quickly recovered, scrambled to her feet, and sprinted into the living room. Her father was sitting in the recliner in his pajamas and slippers, calmly sipping out of a steaming coffee cup while reading the morning newspaper. Sweat poured down Lynn's face.

"Dad, what's going on?"

"Just the birds," her father answered without looking up.

"Wha-" Lynn gasped breathlessly. She walked back into the kitchen and her eyes widened with amazement.

Her mother was pounding on the window pane and yelling. "You! Get off him right now!"

"Come on now, Christine!" Lynn's dad yelled from the other room.

"Mom!" Lynn yelled. "What are you doing?"

"That rotten blue jay came back again," her mother seethed, hitting the window with her fist. "He's trying to steal the robin family's food!"

Lynn gasped. There was no Hookman at the door. She nearly broke her neck and had a heart attack over a stupid bird squabble.

"Oh, for God's sake, Mom!" Lynn fumed. She spun on her heel and stormed back upstairs.

*

"OH MY GOD!" Madison exclaimed as Lynn set her lunch tray next to hers and sat down at the long, wooden table. "What the *heck* happened to your hair?"

It was warm and sunny outside, so the lunch monitors allowed the fifth and sixth graders to eat their lunches outside.

Lynn flicked a quick glance toward the fields behind the school. The tall stalks of wheat gently swayed in the light spring breeze. She sighed. She'd never be able to look at the fields the same way again. She turned around in her seat and picked lamely at her carrots with her fork.

All her friends were staring at her with their mouths hanging open, but Lynn discovered she didn't really care. "The witches happened to my hair, that's what," she finally answered.

Her friends exchanged looks.

"Witches?" Devon repeated with a frown.

Lynn leaned over Madison so that she could see her. "Yeah, Devon. Witches. You know, they fly past the moon on Halloween night with black cats on their broomsticks? I needed information. Maddy recommended I speak to the farmhouse witches. They live right over there," she indicated, pointing down the hill and into the fields beyond.

She realized she was speaking bluntly almost to the point of being rude, but that didn't bother her either.

She was too angry to worry about being polite. And she was doing everything she could to avoid looking at Madison.

"To get the information," Lynn continued on, "one of the witches cut off all my hair. Then, she turned one of the other witches into a frog. Me and Zachary were thrown into the basement with a nine headed creature called a Hydra. Bet I'll get that definition right next time I take a mythology test," she added with a laugh.

"Sounds like quite the adventure," said Devon.

"We killed the beast by chopping all its heads off and barely made it out with our lives. Finally, we just escaped and climbed up an underground tunnel that led to the soccer field. Over there," she added with a point of her finger.

They remained silent. Andrea looked worried. "Are you feeling okay, Lynn?" she asked, putting her hand on Lynn's forehead.

Lynn swatted her hand away. "Yes, yes. I'm fine," she assured her. She shot Madison a look. *"Now,"* she seethed.

"Well," Maddy added after a long pause. "I don't know why the witches weren't helpful to you like they were me-"

"Know what, Madison," Lynn said, narrowing her eyes. "I don't think they were helpful to you either. I think you just made it up that you talked to them. After all, you still have all of your hair, don't you?"

Madison's face glowed red. "Oh yeah! Well, I think you never saw them and you're just using them to cover up for the fact that you got a really bad haircut!"

Everyone gasped.

"Whoooa," breathed Laurie.

Lynn jumped up from the table and stared at them. "Is that what you all think? Devon?"

Devon's head was low and she looked guilty. "Well...it is a far-fetched story, Lynn."

"Andrea?" Lynn asked again, ignoring Devon. Andrea shot a quick, furtive glance in Madison's direction. "Never mind. Laur-"

"I believe you!" Laurie said enthusiastically, if not downright overzealous.

Lynn smiled and pointed at her. "It's nice to know who your true friends are!"

"Aw, c'mon, Lynn," Devon said. "Don't take it personally. I just never believed in that sort of thing."

Madison folded her arms around her chest. "Well I do and I think Lynn's a liar."

Lynn just about had it. She put her hands on the table and leaned forward so her face was inches away from Madison's.

"What if I could prove it?" challenged Lynn.

The table went silent.

"Hey, even if we don't see anything, it would be fun to have a girl's night out..."

"Where would we be going?" Andrea asked, timidly.

"Oxoboxo Dam Road," Lynn answered firmly. "Midnight."

Lynn visited Zachary for a couple of hours after school, while his parents were still at work. He was still invisible most of the time and it was becoming more and more difficult for Lynn to hear what he was saying. When she could see him, Zachary was pale and his skin felt cold and waxy. The scariest moment was when he almost faded, but not completely, and was stuck for a few minutes between being visible and invisible. During this time, Lynn could see right through his transparent skin to the wall behind him.

Worst, during these terrible minutes, Zachary was wallowing in pain, screaming that the lights were burning him. Lynn couldn't see the lights he was talking about, but she burst into tears as he ran from the room and got sick in the hallway. He returned to the room a moment later, saying he felt better, but Lynn could no longer see him. She helped him into bed and, while she didn't tell him her plan, she did tell him not to worry and that she was going to get some answers.

Lynn snuck out of her house at eleven-fifteen at night and met her friends at the stop sign at the end of Connecticut Blvd.

"Where's Laurie?" she asked, approaching the group.

"She couldn't get out," Devon answered her. "Her mom's still awake."

Andrea analyzed Lynn carefully. "You okay?"

Lynn turned to her. It just dawned on her how her friends probably saw her right now. She hadn't eaten in the past two days, her hair hadn't been brushed in awhile and she hadn't slept at all.

After her visit with Zachary today, she felt almost disconnected from reality as if she were watching her life on television.

"Yeah, I'm great," she lied, but at the edge of hysteria, her words betrayed her voice. "Let's get going."

They started walking down the grassy hill and passed the tree farm on the right side of the road.

"What are we doing once we get to the dam?" Andrea asked, looking nervous.

Lynn was silent for a moment. "Have you guys ever heard of The Hookman?"

Her friends exchanged looks.

"As in The Hookman of Black Ash Swamp? Of course," Madison answered, very matter of factly. "*Everyone's* heard of him."

Lynn turned to her. While she was completely fed up with Madison's know-it-all attitude, she was immensely grateful that they knew what she was talking about.

"Did you know he was once a cruel, vicious captain that killed innocent people to get their land? Huh? Did you know that, Madison?"

Madison ignored her sarcasm. "Yeah. I knew that," she shot back.

Despite the coldness in Madison's voice, Lynn detected a clear notion of uncertainty. She didn't sound like she was telling the truth.

As the group continued down the dark street, Lynn told them about her and Zachary's recent involvement with The Hookman - and his curse. "So now Zach has been marked as his successor," she concluded. "If something isn't done soon, he will become the next Hookman."

When Lynn finished speaking, she looked at each of her friends. Andrea looked scared. Devon looked doubtful. Madison seemed amused.

"Well that has to be the most ridiculous thing I've ever heard," Maddy commented. "You can't just pass a curse onto someone-"

"That's exactly what I thought at first," Lynn immediately interjected. "But, apparently, it can be done. Blott said, 'over the years The Hookman had skilled himself in the Ways of the Other-"

"Blott?" Devon spit out, trying her best not to laugh at the name.

"Yes, Blott," Lynn repeated, agitated. "She's the lead witch."

Madison started laughing. "Was she the witch who cut all your hair off?"

"Yes, Madison. She was the one."

Madison heard the coldness in Lynn's voice and fell silent.

But, although she wasn't laughing out loud, Lynn heard her quietly chuckling and whispering to Andrea who walked beside her. Lynn clenched and unclenched her fists at her sides.

When they reached the dam, they set up their blankets on the right side of the bank. Overhead, they could hear the calm waters of the Oxoboxo River. The forest was abundant with fireflies. The night sky was a deep shade of purple and black, and full of stars.

Andrea warily surveyed the great stone wall of the dam, which rose a couple of hundred feet above them. "So, what exactly are we going to be doing?" she asked, shivering and chattering, even though the air around them was warm.

Lynn turned to her. "We will be contacting the spirits of the captain's old crew. The Oxoboxo River Ghosts."

Madison cleared her throat and then loudly cracked her knuckles. "Just leave the contacting to me. I'm the only one trained in this area. If there are any spirits to conjure up, they will only respond to the voice of a true witch. I will bring them forth. This is why you brought me along as I am the most experienced in this subject."

Oh, she's a witch alright, Lynn thought. Lynn impatiently waved her hand at Madison. "You go right ahead, Maddy."

Madison drew up her knees and placed her arms, palms raised, on her legs, sitting Indian-style on her pink blanket and concentrated. "Oh, Mighty Gods of the Spirit World-"

Devon vigilantly tried to hold in her laughter and snorted instead.

"We welcome you to join with us this night of May...um, what's today's date?" Madison asked, briefly opening her eyes.

"Ninth," Andrea offered, helpfully.

"May ninth of the year nineteen hundred and ninety," she continued on in her best conjuring-spirits-of-the-dead voice. She shut her eyes again and raised her arms up to the sky above the dam that loomed over them. "Break forth from your spiritual binds and come unto us tonight! We are your humble servants. We are here only to learn more about you. In turn, you could learn more about us. Ohh, gracious, all-encompassing spirits of the underworld..."

Lynn's face was bright red and she bit down hard on her lower lip, trying her best not to laugh.

Madison opened up her eyes. "Everyone," she said, thickly. "Hold hands."

Lynn sat across from Madison and she took Devon and Andrea's hands. Andrea's hand was clammy and sweaty.

"Maddy," Devon whispered a moment later. "I don't think this is working."

"You must concentrate," Madison said, slowly. "Clear your mind and dwell only on the wishes of the other side."

"Use the force, Luke," Lynn joked.

Everyone, but Madison, started cracking up.

"Focus," Madison repeated. She drew in three deep breaths into her lungs; exhaled. She rolled her neck to the side and her eyelashes fluttered. Suddenly, her eyes rolled back so only the whites were visible.

Lynn rolled her own eyes in frustration. "This is such horse poop," she muttered.

Madison huffed and they released their hands. "You broke my concentration, Lynn!"

"Sorry," she apologized, although she wasn't feeling the least bit guilty at the moment. "Please continue trying to break through to the spirits of the underworld. I'll keep quiet."

Madison sensed her sarcasm that time.

"Well," she fumed. "Do you think you could do any better?"

Lynn shrugged. "Sure."

She rose to her feet and walked up to the dam. The old, moldy stones were bathed in moonlight and shadows cast out from the odd dimensions of the birch trees that composed the dark forest around them. "Excuse me, ghosts?" she called.

There was some strange pounding noise. The peculiar sound was not like anything Lynn heard before. It came from all around them.

Andrea shrieked. Devon's eyes grew wider as she surveyed the surrounding density. Madison's hand involuntarily clutched her blanket. "What was that?" she asked, fearfully.

"Yes," Lynn continued, calmly. "I need to talk to you about your captain. You know, the one who got you cursed and betrayed you all?"

A piercing shriek came from within the great stone wall. The dam started to glow with a bright blue light.

"Oh, God!" screamed Madison, leaping to her feet. "It's not real! It can't be real!?" she yelled, her whole body quaking.

Lynn turned her head and smirked. The blue lights reflected in her eyes. "Hey, you wanted to see them."

Madison screamed in fear and took off down the road in a blind sprint.

"Right behind you!" shouted Devon, leaping to her feet and following her.

Andrea's eyes were huge now. Lynn glanced at where she was staring and gasped. There were more of them than she thought. In a great rush of white wind, the wailing blue and white creatures flowed over the ridge and spilled down the dam by the hundreds. Watching them, Lynn realized this probably wasn't the safest place to be.

"Get out of here!" she screamed to Andrea.

Andrea stood by Lynn's side, white-faced and shaking in fear.

"Andrea, what are you doing? Run!"

"Not without you," Andrea stammered.

Lynn grabbed her by the shoulders. "Andrea, go! I'll be okay. I need to handle this on my own."

Andrea whimpered, then bolted up the street.

Lynn sensed, rather than saw the ghost that stepped out of the wall and was standing directly behind her. She could feel the cold radiating off it.

By the time all of Lynn's friends were halfway up the steep hill of Oxoboxo Dam Road, they had already begun to forget about the ghosts. Once they turned onto Old Colchester Road, they had forgotten about them completely and exchanged bewildered looks as to their whereabouts.

"What just happened?" asked Devon.

Lynn turned around to face the river ghost. The entity that stood in front of her had a wide, gaping black hole for a mouth; its eyes were two narrow white slits. Its entire body was light blue and shone with a light glowing from within. Each of the hundreds of river ghosts that surrounded her had an aura of white light around them. The wailing was piercing, but it also sounded very sad and lonely.

"Don't you think it's unfair?" she softly asked the one ghost that stood in front of the others. "Why should you remain cursed while he gets to go free?"

The ghost looked remorseful. It spread out its long fingers and reached up to touch Lynn's face.

Everything went black.

*

CHAPTER TEN
The Centaur and The Prophet

LYNN'S EYES OPENED SLOWLY. She was lying on the forest floor. The woods surrounding her were dimly lit from the pale full moon which shone down from the sky. A clomping noise sounded in her ear and she turned her head off to the side. Right in front of her were a pair of horse's hooves.

"What exactly did you think you were doing?" scolded an angry voice above her.

Lynn looked up to see a man attached at the waist to the body of a brown horse. He was well built and handsome, with long brown hair and orange eyes.

He stared upon her with undisguised disdain. "Oh, get up. The Prophet is waiting."

Shakily, she rose to her feet and surveyed the area around them. They were in the forests of Black Ash Swamp Road. She recognized the dirt trail they were walking on. She had rode her bike on it many times before.

"How did I get here?" she asked, puzzled.

"I came back for you after the ghosts left," the centaur retorted. "I guess there must have been something about you they liked. Usually, anyone who confronts them usually meets a much more gruesome fate."

"Thank you," said Lynn.

The centaur ignored her frivolous gratitude and continued to stomp down the dirt trail. "You people never learn. First, you cut down the trees, taking away the baby animals' homes, then your kind likes to stick its noses into places where it doesn't belong."

Now, for the second time in her life, Lynn found herself completely speechless. "I'm sorry."

The centaur sneered and simply ignored her. "Sorry right. They're always sorry. Be sorry when you're dead!"

"I'll take it from here, Kerinse," came a low, grandfatherly voice from the doorway of the old church. Lynn had seen this abandoned church before. It was built over one-hundred and fifty years ago and looked ready to fall apart. Thick vines climbed up the sides of the building and entwined the eaves. The windows were cracked as was the paint.

The centaur shook his head. "Unbelievable," he muttered. Lynn watched him retreat down the path, mumbling complaints to himself. The old man in the doorway chuckled warmly.

"Don't take it personally, dear. Centaurs are, by nature, extremely moody creatures, at best," he informed her. He indicated the doorway with a graceful sweep of his hand.

"Please, come inside," he offered.

Lynn started to step forward, but stopped to think about it. She learned her lesson from her experience with the witches.

The old man appeared kind enough, but you never could quite tell. He was wearing long white robes with a hood covering his head. He had long white hair and a long white beard. He reminded her of a picture she'd seen of England's version of Santa Claus or 'Father Christmas' ...except this elderly man was thinner and didn't have a sack of toys slung over his shoulder. And he also lacked a British accent. Not to mention it was the middle of May.

"Who are you?" she asked, warily.

"I am Prophet," he answered.

"I am Lynn," she greeted.

The forest was dark and shadows fell across his face, obscuring his features, but something about the man seemed strangely familiar. She was so preoccupied with trying to recall how she knew him that she hadn't realized she'd followed him through the doorway until she was already inside. She looked away from his face and gasped.

The confined space inside the small building was impossibly large. It seemed as if they had stepped inside a massive cathedral. The vaulted ceiling was high above their heads and the walls were covered by stained glass windows that were not visible from the outside.

Also, the church was brightly lit in a bright, white light. The light shone off the pews, and there was a large golden crucifix above the altar, whose light bounced off everything it touched.

Lynn stared down at her illuminated hands. The gleaming lighting that shone from her skin wasn't caused by an outside electrical source, for there were no light bulbs she could see.

Everything in the church seemed to give off its own light. She glanced out the windows and saw the dark forest. Inside, it was even brighter than the daylight.

Lynn followed the Prophet down the crimson carpet toward the golden altar, which shone with a brightness of a lighthouse beacon. She squinted against the glare and looked up at the Prophet as he lay his long white fingers on the altar's surface.

Her mouth flew open as she finally got a good look at his face. He had one brown eye and one pale blue eye. "You're Tobias, aren't you?"

The old man chuckled. "Indeed. That is one of the shapes I assume, yes."

After everything that had happened up to this point, Lynn suddenly discovered she wasn't the least bit surprised. "You can change shapes?"

"Yes I can, among my other talents," he said with a wink.

Lynn held her hand up to block some of the light that radiated from the glowing altar.

"Could you, um, maybe turn it down a bit?" she requested.

The Prophet seemed confused. He laughed and waved his hand. The altar light diminished. "I'm so used to it that I forget most people aren't accustomed to seeing spectral-encephalographic waves."

On a good day Lynn could spell 'Mississippi'. "Sorry?" she asked, feeling dumb.

"The light force that everything contains," the Prophet explained. "The aura..."

Lynn heard the word 'aura' from Madison. She said a person's aura is a colored band of energy that surrounds them and it's a powerful key to one's personality. She told Lynn hers was orange, which meant, according to Madison, that Lynn is always in search of an adventure and tends to rebel against authority.

The Prophet stared down into the dim altar and Lynn studied him. "How did you know, back at the camp, about The Hookman? You...tried to warn me, didn't you?" she stammered.

"Yes I did," he affirmed with a nod. "You kids, though - never take the advice of your elders."

"Well, you looked like a five-year-old boy," Lynn pointed out.

"Oh," the Prophet said, laughing. "You're right! I did, didn't I?"

Lynn smiled. "So, how did you know?"

The Prophet rubbed at his long white beard before answering her. "I am a Prophet. I have the ability to foresee future events unfolding."

Lynn watched him carefully. He seemed fine, but something was...*off* about him. It frustrated her that she couldn't put her finger on it. "Whose side are you on?" she found herself asking.

The Prophet seemed confused. "Side? Hmm, side? Well, I suppose I have no *side*. I simply see to it that things happen the way they were meant to happen. The way it was Written for them to happen. Do you understand?"

Lynn didn't. "Written? Written by who?"

"Fate, my child, fate," he replied with a nod.

"Oh, so then what does Fate have to say about what happens to Zachary?"

"Hmm," the Prophet contemplated. He slowly bent down to retrieve something from behind the altar. "To better understand the future, we must know its past."

Lynn gasped as the Prophet placed a glowing silver ball onto the altar in front of them. It was, by far, the most beautiful thing she had ever seen.

"This," the white-haired man indicated, "is the Dome of All Wisdom. It knows All and it can see All. It is inside this sphere that I would like to show you the symbiotic connection between The Hookman and your friend Zachary..."

Lynn stared into the sphere and the air froze around them. The suspended sparkling pieces all loomed above their heads. The lights oscillated within the ball and the colors pieced together to form pictures; which flashed in front of Lynn's eyes in rapid succession.

The evil Captain on his ship, the maid he had a child with, the docking of the ship to unknown land...then a splash of blood; the Indian chief screaming, the dismemberment of a human hand by a serrated blade...the glint of a silver hook, an abandoned cabin with dried blood on its walls...a wooden rocking chair, a wolf with glowing red eyes...a boy cowering in a corner...

"Zachary!" Lynn screamed, tearing her gaze from the sphere. She rushed from the altar and bounded down the white steps. "He has Zach!"

"HAAALT!" cried out the Prophet.

Lynn halted halfway down the aisle and spun around to face him.

Prophet's long white robe billowed all around him and his eyes glowed silver. "You did not hear the rest of the story..." he said, slowly advancing down the steps.

She figured she should hear him out, but...

She slowly backed away from him. He said he didn't have a side. He could be Good or Evil. Even worse, he might very well be both.

"The captain and his maiden bore a son," he confided, stepping forward as Lynn stepped back. "A beautiful baby boy named Samuel. Samuel wed Gertrude, a seamstress, and they had a son they called Lucas. Lucas grew up and married a young girl from Salem, they had a baby boy. They called him William. William's wife gave birth to Mark. At four o'clock in the morning, on this very night, twelve years ago, Mark and Natalie from Oakdale had a boy...they called him Zachary."

Lynn froze mid-step. "What?"

"Zachary Joseph Hartman is actually Captain Reginald Hartman's great-great-great grandson," the Prophet said, stopping in front of her.

"There must be some mistake," Lynn stated in disbelief.

"The time has come for his curse to be lifted. It is Written that The Hookman's Successor will be Zachary Hartman, on the night of his twelfth birthday, when the clock strikes four, in the year nineteen hundred and ninety."

"No," she said. "You're wrong!"

The Prophet's eyes were now glowing silver. With his brilliant eyes and his drab, mechanical voice, the Prophet seemed to be less like a man and more like a machine. "I am never wrong," he claimed. "It is Written and so it shall be done."

"Well," Lynn stated, aware that her attitude might get her into trouble, and painful trouble at that. "I think that book needs to be rewritten."

She slowly turned away from him.

The old man seized her wrist.

The Prophet's white hair flew around him as if electrified. "The events must carry out as Fate would have had it. There is no denying the Great Book-" His grip intensified and Lynn wailed.

Suddenly, the old man looked astonished and blinked in surprise. His eyes faded back to brown and blue and the machine-effect was gone.

Bewildered, he gently released his grip on her wrist and stared deeply at the golden bracelet Zachary gave her.

"Love," he murmured. "There is a Great Love here," he observed.

Lynn studied him as he turned her wrist over to examine the bracelet. "Yes, it's true. I love him very much."

The Prophet lowered his eyes. "This wasn't supposed to happen this way. The Successor was not destined to experience love."

"Love sometimes happens by accident," Lynn said with conviction.

The old man suddenly looked sad. He took both her hands in his. "Look into the sphere."

Together, they looked into the glowing ball. The image split into two different visions. "What you're seeing is two branches of Possibilities for Zachary. Most people only ever have one...every movement they make, every sound they hear, everything they see, leads them down the path that was set for them. In Zachary's case, however, other forces seem to be at work. Fate would have him fulfill the curse. Love would break him free."

Lynn tried to tear her eyes away from the ball, couldn't. In one vision, he and Lynn killed The Hookman. The portion of the ball showing that future turned white. The Prophet pointed down.

"That whiteness indicates the boy's future is open. He could be free and live the life which he chooses."

What Lynn could barely stand to watch was the other side of the sphere.

126

In that horrid, graphic vision, The Hookman cut Zachary's hand off by the wrist and inserted the silver hook into the gaping wound. Zachary fell to the floor, clutching his arm and crying out in agony. The ball then darkened as it showed the passage of time.

In the next vision, Zachary looked to be about fifteen. His piercing blue eyes were cold as he rose from the muddy swamp, swiping his hook through the body of an unsuspecting crow that flew in front of him.

Then he sat down in the mud and used his long, yellow fingernails to shred the bird apart piece by piece. The future Zachary looked up and found Lynn's eyes looking through the ball.

His dark eyes stared into hers and, although his gaze was malevolent, Lynn could clearly see a profound loneliness and despair hidden beneath the surface.

"Stop," she whispered.

The Prophet waved his hand once again and the ball darkened.

Both stayed silent for a long moment. Lynn was shaking and she could not look up. A large tear trickled down her cheek.

"I might be able to help you set him free from The Hookman's Curse. But if I do, Zachary won't remember anything about the events that took place. Do you understand? He can't remember anything. Not even you."

Lynn started to sob. The Prophet lay his hand on her shoulder. "I know it would be difficult but, this is the only way. Everything must be erased. Clean slate. If you carry out my plan to destroy The Hookman, Zachary would be free to live the kind of life he so desires. But he can't remember anything that has to do with The Hookman. The love he has for you will be forgotten."

Lynn looked up and met his eyes. "Could we ever get it back?" she whispered.

"It's up to Fate to decide. But lightning rarely strikes the same place twice."

Lynn's chest felt hollow. She understood what The Prophet was saying, but that didn't ease her pain; the thought of losing Zachary's love forever. But, the alternative was immensely worse.

"Okay," she said, resolutely. "What do I do?"

*

CHAPTER ELEVEN
The Hookman Legacy

LYNN FOLLOWED THE PROPHET'S DIRECTIONS and arrived at the marshlands just after three in the morning. In the distance, across the swamp, she could glimpse a vague outline of The Hookman's cabin, which was engulfed in a thick layer of fog.

She took a deep breath and stepped carefully on the small mounds of withered grass that grew out of the murky waters around her. The swamp floor was bathed in eerie green lights.

She looked down into the foul water and saw thousands of skeletons beneath her feet, lying at the bottom of the swamp.

They were the victims of The Hookman.

Lynn shuddered in revulsion. One of the corpses below her appeared more preserved than the others and she instantly recognized it to be the body they saw at the frog pond.

After what seemed like hours, but was merely twenty minutes, she had reached the cabin and opened the back door.

It was dark inside, almost pitch black, but she could see the rocking chair she witnessed in the Prophet's sphere by the window, framed within a circle of pale white moonlight. The chair creaked as it slowly rocked back and forth, as if guided by something other than wind.

Lynn carefully maneuvered through the room, which was filled up to her heels with the muddy water of the swamp. The stench of mold hit her nostrils as she opened another door and stepped into a darker room.

Sensing an overwhelming amount of danger, she turned away and shut the door behind her.

"Zachary!" she called, hearing only the sound of her own voice echo back at her.

"Lynn!" called out a faint voice.

She froze mid-step and listened. It sounded like the voice was coming from the basement.

Lynn swallowed, feeling her way through the house. Her fingers brushed against spider-webs and decayed wood fell to the floor at her feet.

"Zachary?" In her blinded state, she bumped into a counter and something clattered onto the floor with a dull clang, like a pot. She guessed she was in the kitchen: The Hookman's kitchen!

Gathering herself, she continued on forward and bumped into a door. She reached her shaky hand down and felt around for the knob.

Something hissed behind her and she froze. The hair stood on the back of her neck as she slowly turned around, but all she saw was a thick layer of darkness. When her shaking hand finally enclosed around the wooden knob, she tore the door open, nearly ripping it off its broken hinges.

She bolted down the stairs to the basement, which was dimly lit by the single flaming torch that stuck out of the muddy wall at the bottom of the stairs.

"Lynn!" exclaimed Zachary. He was sitting in a corner with his arms and legs bound by a thick rope. Red marks and scratches covered his face and his clothes were torn and dirty.

"Zach!" called Lynn running across the room.

Zachary's eyes widened. "Lynn, don't move."

Lynn froze as she heard a menacing growl from the shadows behind her. The mangy wolf with the glowing red eyes slowly stepped into the light, staring at her with hatred and blood thirsty malice. Lynn slowly backed away and sat down next to Zachary.

"What-is-that?" she hissed.

Zachary was staring at the wolf, which eased itself to the floor directly in front of them. "It's Remus, the Hookman's dog. He's guarding me until his master returns."

Lynn looked from the wolf to her watch. 3:56. They were about out of time. She started tugging Zachary's restraints and the ropes loosened. "I have to get you out of here."

Remus growled.

Zachary's eyes were like saucers. "We can't. He won't let you."

"The Hell he won't," Lynn said with her usual stubbornness. But she knew Zachary was right.

The wolf looked ready to tear them in half if they so much as moved one step closer to him.

She turned to Zachary and studied his face, focusing especially on his bright blue eyes. The Prophet's plan had to work. It just had to.

She couldn't bear to see her Zachary become the next Hookman and have the tormented life she witnessed in the globe.

Yet, she thought, and her eyes welled up in tears, *even if the plan works, and Zachary is free of the curse, he won't remember me.*

Zachary slowly turned to look at her again. "Oh, Lynn," he said quietly as he put a hand on her cheek. "Please don't cry."

Lynn wanted to confess to him everything the Prophet had told her, but she just couldn't bring herself to do it. She leaned in closer to him and rested her cheek against his so she could whisper in his ear.

"I have a plan to get you out of this, Zachary. But carrying it out has certain...consequences. I want to say this to you now. I hope you have a life filled with love and happiness. I hope-" she trailed off, unable to speak. Her eyes welled up with tears and she cried into Zachary's shoulder.

"Hey," Zachary said. He put his hand under her chin and lifted her face to meet his. "You need to get out of here before he comes back."

"No, Zach. I'm not leaving you," Lynn sobbed. "I have a plan. It will work, trust me."

Zachary tilted his head and smiled at her. "Oh, Lynn," he sympathized. Although his expression was warm, his eyes were dark with despair.

Lynn realized he didn't require the Prophet's sphere to see what the future held for him if the curse was fulfilled.

"I don't think there's any way out of this," he whispered. "As soon as he passes the curse I have to kill myself. That's the only way."

"No, no! Zachary listen, you will survive this. Trust me. I know a way."

Zachary stared into her blue eyes and blinked. "You really do have a plan, don't you?"

Lynn smiled through her tears. "What have I been telling you?"

Zachary smiled. Suddenly, he leaned forward and kissed her right on the lips. It was her first real kiss. Despite tasting salty from their mixed tears, it was the sweetest experience she ever had. The moment, however, was short-lived.

Lynn's watch started beeping. It was 4:00 a.m. They pulled away from each other as the ground in front of them shifted and The Hookman grew from the mud.

At first, they could only see his head. His oily black hair dripped down and obscured his face. And then, his emaciated figure emerged. His skin clung onto his bones and they could clearly see his slimy organs and the thousands of networks of blue veins and arteries beneath his flesh.

His heart was black.

When he rose from the mud, a glint of silver appeared. It was his hook, which he rhythmically tapped against his thigh as if impatient to dig it into fresh flesh. In his other hand, he clutched a serrated blade.

Lynn took a reasonable guess that it was the same blade he was dismembered with years ago. The very same blade he planned to use to cut off Zachary's hand to perform the affliction that was cast upon him.

Lynn and Zachary held hands and scrambled to their feet. Remus moved away so his master could easily get access to them. The mutated wolf bared his teeth and almost seemed to be grinning.

She finally relinquished her boyfriend's hand and stepped forward. She took a deep breath and stood directly in front of The Hookman who was completely visible, save his feet.

The Hookman loomed over her and slowly raised his head. Oily black mud dripped from the pits that were his eyes and his disfigured mouth spread into a grin.

The blood practically froze in Lynn's veins as she found herself unable to move. She felt frozen to the core, almost paralyzed.

The oily black eyes of The Hookman stared into hers and seemed depthless. Layers of Hell enveloped before her like the slow blossoming of a thorny rose bush. She lost all sense of space and time. It felt like she would never stop falling. Fire and smoke surrounded her, as did the souls of the damned. There was so much suffering, so much pain...

Vaguely, she was aware The Hookman was squeezing her neck. From far away, she could hear Zachary yelling her name. The images of demons receded and the image of two glowing Indian girls appeared in its place. Together, they walked through an endless field of fire, and they smiled at her. A bright light flashed before her eyes and she was violently thrown to the ground.

Zachary was now standing right in front of The Hookman. Lynn struggled to get her breath after The Hookman released his grasp, distracted by the presence of Zachary. She shook her head from side to side, trying to ward off the leftover images projected in her mind by The Hookman.

Following the Prophet's instructions, she took off her golden bracelet, which was a symbol of everything she and Zachary symbolized.

The Hookman opened his mouth wider than humanly possible. A deafening shrill cry erupted from his throat. Zachary doubled over with his hands covering his ears.

Lynn's eyes narrowed. She scrambled back to her feet and stepped in front of Zachary.

"This is *Love*," Lynn shouted. She reached up and pressed the golden chain to The Hookman's oily cheek. His eyes widened and he expelled a piercing scream as his skin peeled away from the contact with the bracelet.

"Love is something true. Something that you will never understand," Lynn intoned, stepping forward as the Hookman backed away from her.

There was a horrible hissing sound as his skin oozed down his face and melted into his neck.

"Love is the greatest power on Earth. Greater than evil and greater than hate. Me and Zachary have true Love and you-" she spat out, pressing the bracelet harder against his cheek. "-will not take it away from us."

Zachary watched in stunned amazement as The Hookman dropped to his knees, screaming in agony. A dreadful howling sounded from the corner of the room.

Lynn looked up to see Remus writhing on the ground, surrounded by a fizzing steam. She was so distracted by the mournful cries of the wolf that she didn't even notice The Hookman lifting his hook high above her chest.

"Noo!" screamed Zachary as he leaped up and seized the creature's wrist, stopping the deadly instrument in mid-air.

Lynn's eyes were huge as she turned around and saw the hook had come mere inches away from striking her heart.

As they struggled, The Hookman sneered at Zachary. "It's your turn," he stated.

Zachary raised his eyebrows and gave him a knowing smile. "Not this time around."

While the creature was focused on Zachary, Lynn had torn his hook from his wrist. Now she held it poised above the creature's chest.

The Hookman twisted his head around to face her and Lynn saw fear in his black eyes. For the first time, there was fear in his eyes!

"NO!" he screamed.

Wincing, Lynn closed her eyes and plunged The Hookman right into his black heart with his own hook.

The serrated blade dropped from his fingers as The Hookman released a primal scream. His skin withered and folded in on itself.

Within a few seconds, what was once Captain Reginald Hartman crumpled to the floor into a heaping pile of ash.

The room was still and silent. Lynn squeezed her eyes shut while her hand clutched the silver hook. Gently, Zachary pried the hook from her rigid fingers and tossed it to the floor.

"Is he finally dead?" Lynn asked in disbelief. She had killed insects before, but nothing larger than a spider. But yet, this feeling was ten times worse!

"He's gone," Zachary answered, taking her in his arms.

They observed the blackened remains at their feet. After some time passed, they went outside and stood on the porch of the Hookman's cabin.

Lynn tapped the silver hook against her thigh and started humming, *O' Susanna!*

Zachary laughed. "You are a weird one, Lynn Strauss."

"I know," she agreed.

"But that's why I like you."

The morning sun was just beginning to rise above the hills in the east, illuminating across the marshlands in a soft, orange glow.

"Look!" Lynn exclaimed, pointing toward the swampy waters. The white spirits of the deceased rose up from the marshes by the thousands then disappeared into the sky above.

Zachary watched the ascending spirits. "Well, I guess they-" In mid-sentence he was cut off as a blinding light struck him. The pain was intense. He crouched over with his hands on his temples.

The vision he saw struck his mind with such a ferocity that he would have fallen over if Lynn had not caught him by the arm.

"Zach!" she cried out. "What is it?"

There was a black creature descending into a muddy floor; another strange multi-headed beast flailing its arms. Three old woman were moving around a room at a frantic speed. And they were running backwards...

Zachary was exhausted as he sat down on the porch and collapsed.

The images were gone.

He put his head in his hands. "I-I don't know what just happened," he stammered.

Lynn sat next to him and put her hand on his arm. His face was pale white. "Are you okay?"

"I don't know," Zach answered, truthfully. He was staring at the wooden floor beneath his feet. He couldn't explain to Lynn what he saw in the vision, but he had the awful feeling that he forgot something. Something very important...

Zachary slowly raised his head to look at her and blinked in surprise. Suddenly, it came to him that he wasn't where he was supposed to be. Just a few moments ago, he was talking to Bob about dodgeball at school. Bob was talking about taking him to the nurse and he was just about to open the door to go out onto the back lot...there was a flash of light and...now he was here. It appeared to be early morning.

There were swampy waters all around them and, directly behind him was an old, rustic cabin.

"How did this happen?" he faltered, feeling more than a little bewildered.

Lynn's hand was trembling as she placed her arm around his shoulders.

"It's okay, Zachary," she assured

Zachary looked at her with his mouth open.

"How did I get here? What just happened?"

Lynn's eyes were watering but she held back.

Everything was happening just the way the Prophet said it would.

Time was running backwards for Zachary.

He was already starting to forget.

"Come on," she coaxed, gently helping him to his feet. "Let's go home."

Lynn and Zachary reached the road by 5:30. They were filthy, scratched up, and wholly exhausted. Zachary was quiet during most of the walk back to the manor. Lynn felt his hand loosen on hers and she turned to him. His light blue eyes were unfocused and he appeared disorientated, as if he were staring at something she couldn't see.

Lynn squeezed his hand and he blinked from his reverie to look at her face. For a moment, he appeared confused - as if he didn't quite know where he was or what she was doing with him. Then, he put his arm around her shoulders.

"Are you okay?" she asked.

Zachary did not answer her. He could barely keep his eyes open. Lynn waved her hand in front of his face but didn't get any reaction. He seemed to be in another place.

"Pick a pocket..." he whispered.

Lynn couldn't bear it. She turned her head away and stared down Chapel Hill Rd. Fog clung to the pavement and rolled away from them into the forests that surrounded the road. She looked up into the gray sky as she could no longer fight back the tears.

Twenty minutes later, they reached Vermont Road. Lynn helped Zachary up to his front porch. Now, as she stared into his eyes, he seemed to be in another time in their past. He was perplexed.

"Zachary," she said, gently grasping his hand.

"Oh my god, what in the devil was that?" he whispered.

For a moment, Lynn was confused. Then, she remembered those were his precise words after he freed her from the snapping turtle at Oakdale Pond. Any minute now, all memory he had of her would be lost. "Zachary," she repeated, tearfully.

He stared right through her at a point in their past. His eyes widened as he caught a glimpse of the red eyed monster behind the girl he dove in the water to save.

Lynn put her hands on his cheeks. "Zachary, please," she sobbed.

Suddenly his hand was on her arm. He slowly looked down and his eyes met hers directly. The sunlight broke through the abysmal clouds above them and illuminated down on him so his blue eyes sparkled. Lynn stared at him as if for the first time. She was surrounded by water. There was a snapping turtle attached to her leg.

The brown-haired, blue-eyed boy she'd met at the surface was holding her hand. His piercing eyes bore into hers and, for a moment, she was certain she was dead and she was gazing into the eyes of an angel. She smiled at the boy.

"Stay with me, okay?" she whispered.

He gave her a reassuring smile. "Always."

A white brilliance surrounded them. Lynn felt like she was floating while the white winds gently flowcd around them. The force swept up between their fingertips and softly separated their hands.

Lynn watched Zachary slowly fading away. "No," she begged, but the forces would not listen.

Lynn reappeared in her bedroom a moment later. Alone in the dark, she clutched Bedtime Bear close to her chest and cried until it seemed she had no tears left to shed.

*

CHAPTER TWELVE
The Return of Remus

LYNN WALKED OUTSIDE to meet her friends on the swings when it was time for recess the next day.

"Where in the heck did you go last night?" Madison scolded.

"Yeah, where were you?" parroted Andrea.

Lynn was silent as she sat next to Madison on the end swing, surveying the playground.

"Sorry, couldn't get out, Oh well," she replied, dispassionately.

"Or um maybe you chickened out?" suggested Madison.

Lynn just ignored her. "Have you guys seen Zachary?"

"Zachary Hartman?" Madison squealed.

Lynn glared at her, but then realized that her friend had genuinely forgotten that Zachary was her boyfriend. "Yes, Zachary Hartman," she said, quietly.

"There he is!" Andrea stated, pointing across the playground.

Zachary was standing on the bottom rung of the jungle gym and he was laughing at something Steve said from the top.

Lynn took a deep breath, lifted herself from the swing, and started to walk over to them.

"What is she doing?" squeaked Madison from the swings behind her.

As Lynn drew closer, Zachary looked up and met her eyes. He smiled at her as she approached him. "Hi," he said as she stopped and stood in front of him.

"Hi," Lynn said, studying his face.

There was a silent moment and Zachary tilted his head, looking pleasantly confused.

"Zach, she's a fifth-grader!" hissed Steve from the top bar.

Steve and Bob started laughing.

Lynn ignored them and stared at Zachary. "Is everything alright, Zach?"

He just stared at her. "Uh, yeah. Sure."

Lynn searched his eyes, looking for any sign that he recognized her, but she saw nothing there.

"Is something wrong?" he asked, concerned.

Lynn felt tears threaten behind her eyelids. "You...you don't remember me, do you?"

Zachary shook his head, genuinely baffled. "Uh, no. I'm sorry."

"That's okay," she whispered.

She felt despair wash over her and the tears she was trying to hold back all flooded down her cheeks. She unclasped the golden bracelet from her wrist and reached down to take his hand.

Zachary watched her as she turned his hand over and gently placed the bracelet into his palm.

With her eyes downcast, she turned and then walked away.

Zachary slowly looked down and stared at the bracelet the girl had left behind for him.

"Lynn?" he called after her.

Lynn froze mid-step. She felt her heart surge with hope and she turned around to face him.

"Your name's Lynn...*Strauss*, right?"

His adorable smile broke her heart. He knew her name but he didn't know her.

"Yes," she answered. "I am Lynn Strauss."

Lynn went on a night run some two months later. It was 10:00 and raining. Her sneakers plodded into the pavement, sending splatters of puddle-water around her ankles.

She was totally drenched and her socks were all soggy, but that didn't slow her down. She ran down Massachusetts Rd, then took a right onto Pennsylvania, and swung a left onto Connecticut Blvd. She was near her elementary school now and stopped to catch her breath.

She stretched her tired muscles. She enjoyed running. It was relaxing. She'd been practicing a lot and her muscles weren't as tight as they were before.

If she continued to run, then she might be a valuable member of Murphy Junior High's cross country team. *But it would take a lot of practice,* she told herself as she reached her leg up behind her. And no slacking off. Florence Jo Henderson wasn't a slacker.

Lynn was stretching her arm to the side when she heard the familiar growl behind her. Her skin went cold as she looked over her shoulder.

There was nothing there.

The orange streetlamps that lined the road cast circles of orange light onto the wet pavement and it was into this light that the transparent dog stepped forward, holding the dead squirrel in its locked jaws.

The wolf was two streetlights away from her. His bright fiery eyes bore into hers as he chewed on the meat of the dead animal. Lynn tilted her head and continued to return his stare.

The initial panic at seeing the dog wore off. She suddenly felt very calm. Since The Hookman was gone, his dog was powerless and could not hurt the living.

Lynn wasn't exactly sure how she knew this information, but she was as sure of this fact, as she was of the ground beneath her feet. Maybe she knew because the Hookman's hook was still in her possession; no longer a killing instrument, but a rare souvenir stashed away in the back of her closet.

Lynn could see right through the wolf. Being mostly dead, he was only able to feed on the dead. Because of his master's curse, he was condemned to live forever in a barely visible state.

Remus stepped forward, dropping the dead squirrel into the pool of light. As soon as Remus stepped out of the light, she could not see him at all anymore.

"Hey, stupid!" yelled a voice behind her. Lynn recognized it even before she turned around.

It was Tyler Wahrman with his ever-faithful followers, Richard Crawford and Tim Campbell.

She rolled her eyes and turned around to face them. They were going into high school next year, but that didn't stop them. Some people were just bullies for life. They stood ten feet away from her, looking ready for battle.

"So you got any money for me, sweetheart?" Tyler sneered.

"Have you met my new dog?" Lynn inquired with a casual sweep of her hand to the shadows behind her.

"What are ya talkin' about, freak?" Tyler spat, stepping forward and slamming his fist into the palm of his hand. "There is no-"

It was then that Remus stepped into the pool of light and stood next to Lynn. Muddy, swampy water dripped from his mangy coat and decaying flesh. His eyes glowed with a fierce orange light as he stared up at the boys and growled, baring a series of razor-white fangs. Although the dog was transparent, the look was very effective.

Apparently, the boys weren't aware that the dog couldn't hurt them. They were white-faced and shaking in fear. Tim Campbell wet his pants.

"Remus," Lynn sneered. "Sic 'em, boy!"

The wolf dog barked and lunged forward. The Manor Boys screamed as one and took off into the night, closely followed by a nearly dead beast from Hell.

Lynn just smiled and walked down the street, using only the glow from the orange streetlamps to guide her back home.

~ *THE END* ~

About the Author

Hayley Bernard is a short story author, a novelist and poet. Several of her short stories have appeared in **SNM Horror Magazine,** including *Severed Ties*, *The God Worshippers,* and *Black House*. When she's not frightening readers with her writing, she could most likely be found dancing the night away with friends at a hot Philadelphia club...or just painting calmly in her studio apartment. She resides in Pennsylvania by way of Connecticut. This marks her debut novella as an author.

Thank you for purchasing this novella.

Inscription Page

Made in United States
North Haven, CT
05 May 2023

36276826R00089